WHEN YOU ARE STUCK IN A RUT & NEED A MOTIVATIONAL KICK IN THE BUTT - READ THIS BOOK!

Praise for *When You Are Stuck in a Rut &*
Need a Motivational Kick in the Butt

"One of the most riveting and life-changing books ever to hit the global book market. Every author, every story could be its own blockbuster movie. I urge all to read this book—it will empower you and help you to never give up!"

> —Mr. Matt, global master info
> marketer and Internet SEO guru

"Jennifer Nicole Lee is known for being a motivational powerhouse. This latest project has totally changed the entire landscape of self-help books! This is a must read!"

> —Marli Resende, top world
> saleswoman of Gucci Worldwide

"I urge all to read and read again! There are so many layers and positive messages in every story. This will be the best money you ever spend on a book!"

> —Dr. Joe Vitale, New Age healer, best-
> selling author, and top teacher of *The Secret*

"This may just be better and more powerful than the *Chicken Soup for the Soul* books. As I read this book, all the colorful stories of people going from victim to victor shouted out to me to help me become stronger and more determined not to let life's failures get me down."

> —Priscilla Branco, owner and CEO of Up Vibe

"This book is an excellent natural antidepressant. Everyone will grow spiritually so much after reading this timeless motivational self-help classic."

> —Jack Canfield, best-selling author of the best-
> selling book series of all time, *Chicken Soup for the Soul*

WHEN YOU ARE STUCK IN A RUT & NEED A MOTIVATIONAL KICK IN THE BUTT READ THIS BOOK!

World's Most Inspirational Stories to Help You to Believe & Never Give Up!

JENNIFER NICOLE LEE

Medical Disclaimer

The information in this work is in no way intended as medical advice or as a substitute for medical counseling. This publication contains the opinions and ideas of its author. It is intended to provide helpful and informative material on the subjects addressed in the publication. It is sold with the understanding that the author and publisher are not engaged in rendering medical, health, psychological, or any other kind of personal professional services in the book. If the reader requires personal medical, health, or other assistance or advice, a competent professional should be consulted. The author and publisher specifically disclaim all responsibility for any liability or loss, personal or otherwise, that is incurred as a consequence, directly or indirectly, of the use and application of the contents of this book. Before starting a weight-loss plan, a new eating program, or beginning or modifying an exercise program, check with your physician to make sure that the changes are right for you.

ISBN: 0692234543
ISBN 13: 9780692234549

DEDICATION

This book is dedicated to *you*—you reading this right now! May it fill you with positive energy and supercharge your spirit. I also dedicate this book to all the amazing angels who have shared their personal stories of overcoming hardship. You never gave up, you never gave in—*and you made the decision to win!* I believe in *you*!

SPECIAL THANKS FROM BEST-SELLING AUTHOR JENNIFER NICOLE LEE

During the writing of this book, I went through a separation and divorce after being married for over sixteen years. I want to thank all of my fans and fitness friends from around the world for their constant love and support to keep me strong and help me to always believe and NEVER GIVE UP! I believe in angels and blessings, and by the grace of God, Edward and I are much happier, and even closer as friends. We both thank you for your constant prayers as we stay committed to the success of our two kings, our sons Jaden and Dylan.

TABLE OF CONTENTS

FOREWORD

When I was asked to write the foreword for this book, I was taken aback at the opportunity to be a part of groundbreaking history in the making. I cried, and then I panicked! Who was I to be entrusted with such an important task? What was I going to say?

As I began to read the pages of this book, I was reignited by the inspiration and the fire I felt the day I first read Jennifer Nicole Lee's personal story. To say that this book is just a collection of weight-loss success stories would be a disservice. *When You Are Stuck in a Rut* is much more than that. Within each page, the message of "never give up, never give in" is loud and clear. The idea of the law of attraction—that thoughts become things—resonates throughout each story. It is impossible to read this book and not be inspired by each individual journey. The women in this book have bared all, sharing very personal accounts of their vulnerability, their hurt, and their disappointments, but most important, their tenacity to keep moving forward. All have shared with the hope and purpose of paying it forward, of enlightening and empowering every reader to know that you can absolutely take back control of your life. No matter your age, gender, weight, physical challenges, or circumstances, you can go from victim to warrior to champion to mentor.

With all that being said, we, the women who have shared our stories and our personal triumphs, are not the heroes; we are now the mentors. And we applaud *you*—the reader! You have become your *own* hero. You have taken the first step to changing your life. Thoughts become things. Therefore, choose to feed your mind, body, and spirit with this collection of triumphs and reminders to *never give up*. Step out in faith and read this book. We applaud you for having the courage and presence of mind to use these stories to empower you with fortitude, whether you are just starting your journey or need that push to keep going. We believe in you!

—Christine Jackson,
top sales rep, master global marketer,
and corporate consultant

ACKNOWLEDGMENTS

This book is dedicated to the millions of JNL fans and fitness friends around the world. You all simply amaze me. The energy you give me is a big sign that what I do day in and day out really does matter, and that my books, programs, and fitness products really have helped you not only to achieve your fitness goals, but also to exceed them. Being a super fitness model, it is my duty to fill the void left wide open by the wellness industry. My niche market is women who want to look like a fitness model even if they aren't one. For the busy college student, the real-life working mom, the nine-to-fiver, the CEO, and the office executive—now you hold in your hands the blueprint for achieving that coveted fitness-model physique! Your never-ending e-mails, phone calls, and letters of love, light, and encouragement, telling me how I helped you achieve your fitness goals, are the fuel to my fitness fire. I am successful because *you* are successful. I know in my mind, body, and soul that if I am able to motivate just one person to be better, then I have succeeded in life. To know that I am influencing millions on a global level gives me sheer, priceless joy.

So I thank you, and I dedicate this book to you. I believe that we all share a common goal: to increase the quality of our lives through health and fitness. Your desires for greater well-being have provided me with a continuing source of motivation. May my Bikini Model Diet Program awaken the dormant athlete in you and strengthen you mentally, physical, and spiritually. May my fitness expertise, insight, and motivation help you achieve your life goals and your fitness goals while bringing you health, healing, and happiness.

I thank the entire book and management team who helped me create and design this book as a key to unlocking the unlimited potential of my fitness friends.

Also, I dedicate this book to my foundation—my two kings, my two strong and handsome princes—Jaden and Dylan.

To my VIP clients at www.JNLFitnessStudioOnline.com: I live for training you online! I love to see you all, from every corner of the globe, working out online. From Brazil to Germany, from Switzerland to Canada, from the United Kingdom to here in the United States—it's just amazing to see how we all are able to connect online and enjoy a solid, kick-ass JNL Fusion workout together. I always take my training sessions seriously and focus on pushing my body to the next level.

This dedication would not be complete without mentioning Queen Tara of Tara Productions. I admire you for your passion in life, for your sweet spirit, for being a mentor to me, and for mastering the art form of the ultimate infomercial. You are a true talent and genius! And to Princess Skye Madison, who is such a regal, poised little angel. You are so blessed to have Tara as your mother, and we are so lucky to have you in our lives. You are a joy to work with, and I thank you for always making our productions go so smoothly.

To the dream team, each and everyone person in our JNL family, who are the brain and heart of the JNL Fusion fitness family: thank you for believing in me and always working so hard to give our fitness family the best ever!

And thank you to my best friend, Marli, for believing in me. You are my life coach, always there to listen to me, support me, and help me find my way. Every day, you make my life richer, better, and worth living. You are an angel to me, and I appreciate you. Words cannot express my gratitude for all that you have done to help me and support me.

Last but not least, a special big thanks to all of my team members at ProSupps. I love being the official spokesmodel as well as the global marketing consultant. Let's keep kicking ass!

Smile,

JNL

"Never give up!"
—Jennifer Nicole Lee

For more inspirational books, fitness support, and self-help books, please visit www.JNLBooks.com.

CHAPTER ONE

Never Give Up—Believe
by Jennifer Nicole Lee

The real JNL story revealed!
What you don't know about me will
inspire you to never give up—believe!

Many of you know the Jennifer Nicole Lee in the photos, on the magazine covers, and in the media. But most of you have seen only a small glimpse of my entire personal story. It's like reading only the last chapter of a book about an overweight, depressed housewife who takes life by the horns by losing weight and enjoying her newfound freedom and success.

But few people know the early chapters of my life. The third of four children, I had two older sisters and a younger brother. I grew up in a small, racially charged Tennessee country town, an outcast due to my olive-toned Italian skin, a color passed down to me by my immigrant parents. I had no self-confidence or strong sense of identity.

Nor do most of you know that I was raised in poverty. My parents never had enough money to take care of us all, and later my mom struggled to raise four kids by herself. There was always more month left at the end of the money. It was embarrassing to be the only girl at my elementary school who received free lunches through the welfare program, but I was grateful for a well-balanced, tummy-filling lunch at midday, the only real meal I enjoyed. If it weren't for food stamps and provisions received from my family's church, I really don't know if I would be here today, let alone as a successful survivor.

Fed up with my dad, my mom finally got up the nerve to file for divorce when she was pregnant with her fourth child, my little brother. I was only a few years old, and my earliest memories of my parents are of them fighting and my mom kicking my dad out of the house. I witnessed so much hate, anger, resentment, and negativity at such an early age. It was like an episode of *The Sopranos,* but it was for real.

After the divorce, my mom and we kids were left to fend for ourselves. At times it was so bad that we survived on government cheese, big jars of spaghetti sauce, and white rice. But boy, did my mom do her best. She worked three jobs to make ends meet. My older sister Rosalinda posed as our mother many times when our real mom was out working. Rosalinda took charge of the household while Mom cleaned houses, worked at the grocery store, and even babysat to make a little extra cash.

Under these harsh circumstances, exercising and eating right were the last things on our minds. Our focus was constantly on just keeping our heads above water and surviving for another day. Our holidays, birthday parties, and celebrations were not what most children experience. I can recall many Christmases when the tree was barren, with no presents underneath.

One Christmas I got lucky—my mom was able to afford a doll for me. I badly wanted the gift to be from Santa Claus, so I wrapped it with my own little hands and labeled it, "Love you, Jennifer, from Santa Claus." I placed it under the tree and was excited to see a present there, even though I was the one who wrapped it and knew very well what was inside. I was so joyful to know it was waiting for me to open on Christmas morning. It made me feel safe and secure—normal, like the other families I knew at school.

Yes, times were tough. But these tough times and tough experiences were not tougher than my family or me. My spirit was tougher, and I'm here to tell you about it. Even though my mom could not provide a stable and financially secure childhood for us, the one important life lesson she taught me was to never give up!

Being raised in a small home with only two bedrooms and one bathroom for five people was extremely hard. We had no money for entertainment, movies, traveling, or fun days out and about—and forget about vacations. Sometimes the TV was my biggest escape from my harsh, cold reality. My favorite memories are of watching Jane Fonda and the other fitness experts and beautiful aerobic teachers. They were so happy, so strong, so confident and sure of themselves. They exuded the kind of positive, life-changing energy I needed to see at that desperate time of my life. Jane Fonda and the others were so in tune with their bodies; they were confident and in charge. I loved the strong, captivating, positive auras they had about them. This was what I wanted to be! This would be my journey in life. I wanted to provide hope, to motivate others to never give up. I wanted to inspire other women and young girls who were also silently suffering in their own lives and their own bodies. This was my mission—*is* my mission—and I will never give up!

Just as my role models gave me the strength I needed when I was weak, destitute, and desperate, it's now my turn to pass the torch of motivation, inspiration, hope, and faith to other women who need this message now as badly as I did then.

Allow me to fast-forward my story. Before I gave birth to my healthy, happy, gifted sons, Jaden and Dylan, whom I love so much, I suffered a life-threatening miscarriage. I was just over three months along in my pregnancy, and we were so excited about this little special spirit God had blessed us with. Edward and I were traveling in Kingston, Jamaica, where he was born and raised.

Jamaica is a special island. It is a coin with two sides, and its duality is mystical. It's a beautiful country filled with one-of-a-kind energy, what the natives call "irie." It has gorgeous mountains, music, and people. But it's also a third-world country where there is much poverty and suffering. Take one wrong turn, and it can become completely dangerous and deadly in an instant! Trust me, it's not a place you would want to be if you were faced with a life-threatening medical emergency—as I was.

And it started to happen: I began to bleed. I cannot tell you the rush of horror that flushed through my body when I saw the blood-stain on my clothes. I knew right then and there that my little baby's life was in danger, and so was mine.

I had Edward rush me to the ER that, sadly enough, was the equivalent of a dressed-up garage with no air conditioning. The next few hours would be among the most unforgettable of my life, second only to the birth of my two sons. My body just let go, and I went cold, releasing the lifeless body of my unborn baby. Outside it was raining hard, and the rain seemed to be beating down the ceiling of the old medical building. I was lost, scared, and confused. All this mayhem and sadness had happened so suddenly.

Following the miscarriage, I needed to have a dilation and curettage procedure. Seeing that I could not handle the pain, they gave me anesthesia to put me to sleep. When I woke up, Edward was lovingly by my side. Weak, exhausted, drained, and terribly saddened by this unexpected miscarriage, I could only muster the strength to peer out the small window of my cement-block room. There was no glass in the window, only vertical metal bars, like a prison.

In the heat and humidity of my humble hospital room, I saw something special shining in the bleak dark sky following the pounding rains. *It couldn't be,* I said to myself. It was the most beautiful full rainbow my eyes have ever beheld! The colors seemed so bright and real, and the arc was so huge, I felt as if I could have reached right through the metal bars and grabbed it. That rainbow was a message I needed to receive. It represented a promise, a guarantee from my creator that "this too shall pass," that I must have hope, be strong, and let go and let God.

God comforted me in an instant when I had started to wonder, "Why me? What did I do to deserve this?" The rainbow he showed me was a witness that God knows best, all the time, and to trust in him. It was a sign that after every storm in life comes a shining rainbow, a promise of happiness and peace.

Just a short three months later, God blessed Edward and me with a new pregnancy. Nine months later, I gave birth to a healthy, happy baby boy named Jaden. And just one year after Jaden was born, we were blessed with a second baby, Dylan.

Even though I joke that I was pregnant, breastfeeding, or somewhere in between for a good five years of my life, being a mom has been the most remarkable experience I could ever imagine. It's also been one of the most challenging. Jaden had many developmental challenges to overcome early in his childhood, including speech difficulties and behavioral problems. It was so bad at one time that we thought Jaden might fall on the autism spectrum. We just could not get through to him, and he could not communicate effectively with us. But the fighter in me, always there, took action! I made it my top priority and duty to get him screened and evaluated.

Heaven worked in our favor. With extensive occupational, speech, and behavioral therapy, Jaden is now one of the brightest, smartest, most well-rounded, happiest boys I could ever be blessed with. As the famous motivational saying goes, "It's not how you start, it's how you finish." This describes my warrior son Jaden to a T. Thanks to caring parents and effective therapy sessions, he has overcome a lot and is now well on his way to major success. He is so smart, successful, and well adjusted at school that he is making straight As, plays the piano like Mozart, and has many friends. He is so intelligent that at his last psychological evaluation, he was off the charts for his age. This is my victory for my son! He is gifted and a genius. I thank God for giving me the strength, energy, and resilience to never give up on Jaden, working with therapists day in and day out to release the genius trapped inside my confused son. Committing to five sessions of speech therapy and four sessions of occupational therapy every week, and then studying with him at home daily, made all the difference in helping him hit all of his major developmental milestones. Again, I urge all of you reading this to *never give up*.

Note: During the creation of this project and book, Edward and I have decided to move on. Even though Edward and I have decided to part ways as husband and wife, we will always remain respectful friends and have been extremely blessed to have our sons and angels Jaden and Dylan. This also goes to show you that life's blessings, challenges, obstacles, and chapters are always to be embraced and enjoyed, no matter how hard or how easy.

CHAPTER TWO

Finding Her Fitness
by Shay Hensley

The brave story of a fallen flight attendant
who became a fitness professional

The Accident

My story is about believing in the power of mind over matter and striving to overcome the physical limits I was told would be permanent after my accident.

I had never stopped to think about how quickly life could change, but it did. My life changed on one overcast day in January 2007. I was a flight attendant, and we had just landed. It had been raining that day, and the skies were dark and cloudy. A chilly breeze in the air suggested it was about to snow. Our aircraft was on the tarmac, and the stairs to the aircraft were down, as we didn't pull up to a Jetway at that airport.

What seemed like any other regular January morning quickly changed. The passengers had already deplaned and gone into the airport. The captain and first officer had also deplaned and were waiting for me at the bottom of the stairs while I finished up with my duties. We were all happy to be back for a layover, and as always, laughter was in the air. I loved my job as a flight attendant, flying the friendly skies. The flight crew was like family. We looked out for one another, took great care of our passengers, and often talked about our families and everyday life over coffee and donuts during our layovers. It was the type of job that was actually quite enjoyable.

7

So there I was at the opening of the aircraft door, ready to head down those stairs. From there, everything happened so fast, yet seemingly in slow motion. My body made the movement to take that first step out of the plane, but my feet remained planted at the doorway of the fuselage. My body went out. In that moment, all I knew was that my face was quickly heading toward the tarmac at the end of the stairs. In my peripheral vision, I could vaguely see the captain and first officer dropping their bags as if to try and catch me, but there was no time. I could hear them saying something, but I couldn't make out the words. Their voices sounded like a movie playing in slow motion. Certain my face was going to hit the tarmac, I instinctively dropped my flight attendant bag, swung my left arm in front of myself, and grabbed the handrail, preventing the face-plant. Unfortunately, I landed on my knees in a fetal position next to the left step, basically crunching my lower spine with the pressure of twelve times my body weight. I instantly felt my shoulder stop the weight of my body hitting the ground. I knew I had just fallen, but I didn't realize how bad.

All of a sudden, everything felt like it was rushing up to me, as my mind caught up on what had just happened. There I was, hanging onto the handrail by one hand in what probably looked like some new form of yoga. I was on my knees, bent over at the spine. My heart raced. *Can I move?* I wondered. *What just happened?* I guess you could say I was in a bit of shock. Then the captain and first officer were by my side, saying how fast it had all happened. They had tried to catch me, but there was no time.

The pain was sharp, like an ice pick being jabbed into my spine and pulled all the way down my right leg and into the toes of my right foot. The pain in my shoulder radiated into my head, and my knees were the color of plums.

I later found out that three screws had worked their way up in the floorboard of the fuselage by the aircraft door. Their function was nothing mechanical but merely cosmetic—they held down the carpet by the door. Fortunately, all passengers and flight crew had deplaned safely. I was the last one to get off the plane. As I began to take my first step out the doorway, the rubber soles of my work shoes got stuck on the screws. Essentially my feet stayed planted as my body went out of the plane.

The Fight

To this day I remember the captain helping evaluate the fall and write up the accident report. I even remember the crass remark of an employee who got me some ice packs and said half-jokingly, "Well, there goes our accident-free safety record. Way to go." I ended up going to the twenty-four-hour urgent care center. Then things got worse. The following day, when I called in to say I was in such excruciating pain that I couldn't work, I was threatened with termination. And that was just the beginning of my story in the recovery from hell—from fallen flight attendant to finding my fitness in life.

The first doctor I saw was in his sixties or seventies and was about to retire. He only took an X-ray of my spine to be sure I didn't break anything. Nothing was broken, and he actually told me, "Take some Advil...the good Lord will heal you." Was he kidding me? I could barely walk from the pain. Everything hurt. His remark took me aback a bit, so I immediately asked for a second opinion, and then a third, this time from a sports-medicine physician. After four months of taking narcotics and muscle relaxers around the clock, I received my first MRI. It showed that my lumbar spinal discs had been crunched during the fall and were compressing all of my nerves, causing what I now know is permanent nerve damage to my leg and foot.

I had always been a fairly healthy gal. I exercised here and there, did my best to eat healthfully, and was inspired by the photos I saw in fitness magazines. I loved going to the gym, hiking with friends, traveling to beautiful beach locations, skydiving, learning to play tennis, and simply trying new things. My life was always pretty active. But now things were different.

For the first two years after the accident, I was being treated for pain management, just to keep the pain level down until I could get surgery. I wasn't making money while off work, and as you can imagine, things were getting tough. I traveled three hours round trip every two to four weeks to see my doctor. My body was being pumped full of medicine, including Neurontin, Valium, Percocet, Vicodin, Lyrica, Ultram, two types of prescription pain patches, steroid patches, on-and-off morphine drips during visits to the ER, and more. This couldn't be all that could help me.

I had a right to medical coverage, but I had to fight for those rights with the insurance company over the course of four years. After having three consultations with surgeons, I knew I needed spinal surgery, but my insurance company would only approve one thing at a time—pain meds, cane, walker, injections, and pool therapy. So what was going to help me actually heal, rather than just mask the pain? In my heart of hearts, I knew if things were going to change, I had to start with belief in myself and the visualization of a healthier, healed body.

There were days when I felt like I was in a downward spiral of misery. The pain. The medicines. The verge of bankruptcy. I was gaining weight from being sedentary. I was using a walker or cane to ambulate. Here in this book is the first time I have ever said publicly that I was at an all-time low. I didn't want to go on. How could I? I was broke—physically, emotionally, spiritually, and financially. My beautiful car had been repossessed, I was on food stamps, I had to move in with family, and I often had to borrow ten dollars just to put enough gas in the car to make it home from my doctor and therapy appointments. Life was so different. It wasn't pretty.

There were numerous trips to the hospital emergency room after I'd peed on myself in the middle of the night while literally crawling and dragging my body across the hallway to try to get to the bathroom. Tears would be streaming down my face and urine streaming into a puddle beneath me because I was stuck, unable to move because the pain was so intense.

The Recovery

It was the day I was in physical therapy, hooked up to a traction harness that kept me partially suspended so that I bore only a few pounds of my body weight while I tried to walk for five minutes, that I asked myself a question. I am not sure what neuron sparked or what phenomenon happened in my brain, but in that moment of being suspended, I wondered, *Is this all there is for me?*

I was tired of the tears. Every day I would cry in pain and in sadness. I felt no reason to really live. Life was broken to me. I was broken. But I still had dreams, visions, and goals. From that day forward, even throughout the most unimaginable pain, I would ask my physical therapist if we could try going just a little bit farther, do just a little more. I started recalling self-help books I had read years ago by authors like Napoleon Hill and Wallace D. Wattles. I knew I didn't want to end up living in pain all of my life, and I made a decision to fight harder than ever to transform and heal. Yes, I still needed surgery, but we had to wait for a court order to force the insurance company to comply with the doctors' orders, and that took almost two years. In the meantime I got epidural steroid injections under fluoroscopic guidance to help keep the pain under control. *Keep on, keep on,* I would tell myself. From my first MRI to my next ten-plus MRIs, my new doctor and I worked together on treatment plans. Little did he know I had big plans for my recovery.

I started reading more magazines and books on fitness and health, personal development, and how powerful the subconscious mind can be. My life had drastically changed, and I figured that if dreaming about feeling good was the only thing that brought me happiness and hope, then I would keep daydreaming about living an active life again. After all, I wanted to reprogram my mind to achieve new things. If I couldn't believe it myself, then my body would not have a way to respond to the new expectations. That was my mindset, anyhow!

Finally, in 2009, the courts awarded me the right to undergo my first spinal surgery. I received lifetime medical benefits for treatment resulting from my injury. This was after accumulating more than $400,000 in unpaid medical bills, and the bills were still stacking up. As you can imagine, the case was appealed. But I was already scheduled for my first surgery.

All I remember thinking before I went in for my surgery was that it was finally happening. I would finally be pain-free! This three-hour procedure took place in June 2009, and it failed miserably.

Three months later I underwent my second spinal surgery, a five-hour procedure. The risks were explained to me: even if it went well, recovery would take years. But I was ready to move forward. I was still dreaming of being pain-free, or at least what I could imagine to be pain-free. So, on August 24, 2009, I underwent a facedown, five-plus-hour spinal surgery in which they placed titanium rods, screws, and cadaver bone in my spine.

After the operation, my blood pressure dropped to 78/47. I had suffered corneal abrasion to both eyes. I had involuntary bowels, and I had an allergic reaction to the surgical tape used to keep my breathing tube in place, my eyes closed, and the sterile dressing adhered to my back during surgery. On top of it all, I had an allergic reaction to the IV antibiotic I was on. The spinal surgery had been even more complicated than they thought—but I made it through. And I was still determined never to give up hope of a full recovery.

In the recovery room at the hospital, I began reflecting on all of the things I had once done and realized how in the blink of an eye, things could change. I already knew that no one was going to look out for me except me. I had once been a thriving gal. I had traveled to places like British Columbia, Ontario, Puerto Rico, and Mexico, and I'd been to almost all fifty states. I had moved across the country, attended black-tie events, and even enjoyed skydiving. I owned my dream convertible car (the one that got repossessed after my accident). My sister and I would go on "sister vacations" to places like the Dominican Republic. We would have family cookouts in the summer. Life was good. I dreamed of enjoying days like that again. I was ready to burn the bridges and do what it took to get back to a healthy, vibrant life. Now here I was, right smack in the middle of the journey. It would be a long recovery after surgery—two more years. But I was in for the long haul, and I was ready to take anything on.

Changing Me, Helping Others

The next two years were when the real healing began. Both physically and mentally, changes began to happen. Determined to get off prescription medicine, I began to eat in a way that would support natural healing. I drank superfood juices, increased my amino acid and protein intake, cut out refined sugars (which I learned enabled inflammation), and started drinking a lot of water. Yes, it sounds silly and superficial, but it was those little lifestyle changes that jump-started my recovery. Four days post-op, I refused all narcotics, and I got off Neurontin for the nerve-damage pain in my leg and foot. The doctors thought I was crazy, but I started training my body to understand the pain and push through it. My diet reduced my internal inflammation, and I began walking more and more. I would walk fifteen minutes here, twenty minutes there. In physical therapy we started using weights to help strengthen my muscles, and I realized how much I loved it. On the days that I got to use the cable machines in therapy, I quickly regained my muscle memory of when I used to work out. Sure, seven-and-a-half-pound dumbbells weren't quite making me a champion, but in my own mind, I was a champion in the making.

"Mind over matter" was my motto, and I knew that if I could begin to make these once-unthinkable changes, there just had to be a way I could do more and give more in life. Life was about overcoming challenges and having triumphant outcomes. I knew I wasn't the only person out there determined to overcome a physical challenge. I kept telling myself that if I could do it and believe in myself, then there were probably others who needed encouragement and guidance. What could I do to motivate and help them? This is where the big dream began.

I am not sure exactly what to call it—maybe a calling. I decided I was going to become a personal trainer. I had dropped out of college in the '90s, so I didn't have a degree, but I studied day in and day out to learn more about my passion—the human body—and how exactly muscles could transform, heal, and gain strength. Eventually I took an eight-week college course, worked a forty-hour internship at a local Gold's Gym, and passed my American Council on Exercise personal training exam and labs with flying colors. But I was thirsting for more knowledge about how nutrition had helped me with my inflammation and healing, so I went on to acquire two nutrition certifications. The first one was in sports nutrition, and the second was from the prestigious International Board of Nutrition and Fitness Coaching. Yes, *this* was my calling in life. I was drawn toward the satisfaction of feeling like I could make a change in others' lives, physically and perhaps even emotionally, too.

In the summer of 2012, I opened a small women's fitness studio, where I was dedicated to helping other women change how they felt about their self-image, reach their personal fitness goals, and work out in a space that was fun, motivational, and challenging. My classes ranged from Daisy Dukes kickboxing to yoga, Brazilian booty class, crunch-time abs, and of course the Fitness Bound Living boot camp classes, all of which made my company, Fitness Bound Living, a success. I have spoken about nutrition at local schools and colleges, and I even taught boot camp to ninety-two people in one day. I can honestly say that people are shocked when they first hear about my accident and how I changed my body. One client even sent me this amazing testimonial about how I helped change her life. I will always remember sharing tears of joy with her.

In July of 2012, I had the honor and privilege to meet Shay Hensley for the first time. I was at a point in my life when I needed to make some very hard health decisions: my weight had spiraled out of control, I was extremely stressed, and my cholesterol was not good. From the first day I met her, my life totally changed due to the motivation and support that I received from her at Fitness Bound Living. I lost weight, learned to handle stress better, and my cholesterol is excellent with no medication necessary! She is always positive and will do whatever it takes to keep you motivated and on track to a healthier life. She genuinely cares about her clients and wants them to succeed; anytime I needed help, all I had to do was ask. Shay has a way of making a healthier life fun and exciting. She is very passionate about helping you to become the best you can be! I know without a doubt that it is her training, support, and positive motivation that has gotten me where I am today with my health and also to love the person I am.

—D. Jenkins

Truly, I tell each of you reading this to always believe in what you want for your life. You might be given a challenge that seems too hard to overcome. But if you never reach for something beyond what you have right here, right now, how will you ever fully know what you can accomplish? Take it from me, a fallen flight attendant with a spinal injury and a lower spine made of titanium and cadaver bone: if I can change my mind-set and be where I am today, then you too can make some changes in your life!

No matter how big or small your challenges might be, just take small steps, and remember that every single step is progress. I believe in you. I do. I might not know you or ever even meet you in this lifetime, but whenever you are doubting yourself or your success, think of me, the Pink Fighter, Fitness Diva, Trainer Shay (yes, I have all of those nicknames), saying, "I believe in your fitness!"

Life is too short not to realize how wonderful and great you are. We all have self-doubt and self-criticism. But we also all have the right to choose a new path. And it starts right here, right now. Mind over matter!

Shay is the founder of Fitness Bound Living, an online fitness and nutrition company that offers e-book fitness programs and also runs social boot camp events. She has been a contributing author for the Urban Athletica, Personal Trainer Magazine, *and the* Villager *newspaper. She also runs Shades of Shay Tanning, the safe, custom-tanning alternative to the sun, which goes hand in hand with living a healthy lifestyle. Shay can be reached at shay@fitnessboundliving.com and www.FitnessBoundLiving.com.*

CHAPTER THREE

Hysterectomy?
What Hysterectomy?
by Carri-Anne Carmichael

I will never forget the day I "became a woman." My mom and aunt made such a fuss over me, but I clearly remember standing there looking at them with a confused smile, thinking, *What now? I'm not sure I like this. I'm not sure I want this!* I was fourteen years old and about to embark on an unwanted twenty-five-year journey. From day one of my period, I never embraced the fact that I had grown up. Womanhood took such a firm grip on me that I never got to understand and enjoy this honor the way I should have. To be totally honest…I hated it! "Why?" you might be asking. I guess there aren't many women who actually like their menstrual cycle, but when you are one of those who suffer the wrath of a number of symptoms on a monthly basis year after year, you just cannot accept that it's something to be valued.

Let me start from the beginning. My period started when I was fourteen, and so did the PMS. I was a moody young woman, very picky, and of course bitchy. People might have seen me as all of these things, but deep down, that wasn't really me. It was my hormones controlling me, my hormones dictating how I felt at certain times. It was definitely not how I wanted to be! Every time my period approached, I was in agony. I suffered tremendous cramps, achy breasts, heavy bleeding that lasted seven days, and of course the infamous PMS moods. Those who don't suffer these symptoms just don't get it, and I've always said I would never wish it upon anyone.

I'm a very outgoing, friendly, bubbly person, and I have a happy, fun personality, if I may say so myself. But I wasn't much like this when it came to that time of the month. I would change into someone else, pretty much like Dr. Jekyll and Mr. Hyde. Looking back today, I can see that I lost a lot of friendships due to my mood swings. It's not something I am proud to admit, but it's something I have had to come to grips with in order to move forward with my life.

Years went by, and I tried lots of different methods to try to help my symptoms: contraceptive pills and injections, homeopathic medications, supplements, and different forms of exercise, to name a few. My life was hard, thanks to this, but I had to be bold and keep going. There was not much else I could do, or at least not that I was aware of. I was also totally unaware that by taking synthetic hormones, I was only making matters worse for myself—not only did my body not accept these hormones, it was actually attacking them.

I met the man of my dreams at the age of twenty-three. Of course, the roller coaster of PMS continued, and it took its toll on our relationship. We had a love/hate relationship and our arguments were fiery, but we were so passionate about each other, we decided to keep it strong through thick and thin, and we got married five years later. We packed up our lives in South Africa soon after and immigrated to the United Kingdom in 2001. We spent almost five years in London and then found our nest in Wales, which is our home today.

The year we bought the house and moved in, I became pregnant. I miscarried the first baby and then suffered a really bad bout of depression for three months, but I became pregnant again three months later. I was thirty-three at the time. Being pregnant was a huge eye-opener, and I realized just how much of a grip my hormones and menstrual cycle had on me. The first trimester was hard going, as is the norm due to the body accepting the changes and hormonal shifts. Then, quite suddenly, a whole new window opened for me, and it was as if I had found that pot of gold at the end of the rainbow. The second and third trimesters of my pregnancy were the most enjoyable time of my entire life to that point. I absolutely loved being pregnant and cherished every moment of it, even when I got uncomfortably big toward the end. I carried my baby with pride and didn't want my pregnancy to end. My life seemed to be put on hold, and I felt it was finally worth living. I hadn't been in such a good place in what seemed like an eternity. Why? Because during these nine fantastic months of my life, I did not have to face a menstrual cycle, and a menstrual cycle did not rule my life. I was able to be me and only me.

My gorgeous, big little boy was born on May 12, 2007. No sooner was he born than I was once again gripped by PMS hell. However, this time it gripped me even worse than it had before. My period started and never ended, or at least it wouldn't have if I had not done something about it. I bled heavily for thirty days, and when I couldn't take it anymore, I saw a doctor, who put me on pills to stop the bleeding. Things settled down a bit, and I became more regular again, but my periods were heavier and still seven days long. I suffered achy breasts again, which did not help with the breastfeeding, and I had to give that up after just six weeks. This really broke my heart, as I had always wanted to bring my baby up on breast milk for as long as possible. I suffered mastitis, and all the time I was weaning my beautiful boy, I gazed down upon his little face, crying bucketloads of tears. I'm quite surprised I didn't drown him in the process.

I plodded on for two years after the birth of my child, with periods that grew increasingly heavier and breasts that would swell to double their size and were so painful to the touch that I could barely hug my child or husband. I had postpartum depression and anxiety attacks. I felt worthless, guilty, tense, and on edge. I had mood swings and was sensitive to rejection, and my feelings were easily hurt. I was angry and irritable, lost interest in usual daily activities, couldn't concentrate, felt lethargic and fatigued, and had increased appetite and cravings for all the wrong foods. I found it hard to get up when I needed to but hard to fall asleep or stay asleep. I felt overwhelmed, unable to cope, and out of control. I gained weight and suffered headaches and joint and muscle pain, among other physical symptoms that I would prefer not to mention here as they are personal. All of these symptoms and more left me less productive and efficient in my daily routine at work and at home. I participated less in hobbies and social activities or avoided them altogether. At least one of the problems mentioned above interfered with my relationships, especially those nearest and dearest to me, like my innocent baby and my less-patient husband, who, after putting up with all of this for so many years, was at the very end of his tether. I often had suicidal thoughts, even though I would not have been able to follow through with any of them. I knew I could never give up because I was a mother and a wife, and my family needed me.

Things got so bad, my husband and I decided to visit the doctor together to ask for help. To our disgust, I was merely offered antidepressants, which didn't address my physical symptoms at all. But we were so desperate, we went with it. The drugs helped make me a slightly calmer person by numbing my feelings of happiness or sadness and just kept me drifting along like a zombie, but all my other symptoms still persisted. My husband couldn't stand my lack of enthusiasm for life, so together we decided this was not the way forward for me, and I gave up the pills six months later. It seemed the doctors didn't really know how to deal with PMS, only how to mask it.

One day, close to a year postpartum, I was waiting for a hospital appointment when I spotted a poster on the wall in the sitting area that read, "Do you suffer with PMS? Most women have a hormonal imbalance and don't even know it!" Well, this hit home, and I decided it was time to take the bull by the horns and do something about it. I joined the National Association for Premenstrual Syndrome (NAPS) and started reading blogs by other women with similar issues. This pushed me into doing more research online to find out as much information as possible to help diagnose my symptoms. I read blog after blog, and through the help of a friend who was suffering the very same symptoms as I and who for many years was diagnosed as bipolar with manic depression, I finally diagnosed myself with premenstrual dysphoric disorder (PMDD).

PMDD is extreme PMS—it's PMS triplefold! You can have it from the start, or you can develop it after the birth of your first child. I had suffered PMS from the start, of course, only to have it become

PMDD after the birth of my little boy. From then on, I researched more information and started a daily record of the severity of my problems so that I could see when my symptoms appeared and how soon before my period so that I knew when to avoid being around people, going out on social events, drinking alcohol, eating sugary foods, and booking holiday weekends away. It just wasn't worth risking how my moods, aches and pains, and other symptoms would affect these events.

I found that my symptoms would start ten days before my period was due, and as soon as my period started, so would the grip these hormones had on me. I would be OK for a maximum of five days while I bled. Toward the end of menstruation, I would suffer two days of the worst symptoms ever. Then, the minute bleeding stopped, I was normal again—and when I say normal, I mean *normal*. I would be the person everyone, including myself, loved being around.

During this time, my periods also increased in length. Although regular, they went from seven days to nine to eleven days and so on, until eventually I was having a period for fifteen days a month. That's half a month! My symptoms increased as well, of course, so I really only had a small window of seven days of being happy and carefree, without the horrible hormonal symptoms. I followed my chart religiously, dreading every month but knowing I had to get myself sorted once and for all, and to be able to approach the doctors with as much information as possible. One thing is for sure: I pat myself on the back for being so tenacious and believing in myself during that time, because without that, I don't think I would be where I am today.

I spent a fortune on visits to a hormone specialist, and I was taking so many supplements that I would have rattled if you shook me. Although the supplements helped me a bit here and there, I still felt awful and suffered tremendously. Finally the day came when I realized I had to rid myself of any future hormonal imbalances if I were to have a life at all. So I approached the doctor with an eight-page essay regarding everything I dealt with on a monthly basis, and I requested a hysterectomy. In October 2012, at the age of thirty-nine, I had a total abdominal hysterectomy and bilateral salpingo-oophorectomy.

I've always been a pretty fit person—not necessarily consistent with fitness, as I've had a lot of ups and downs that got in the way—but I've always enjoyed being active and have done my best to keep fit throughout the majority of my life. Starting from this place of health helped me to heal from my operation fast and well. And there it was—*I was me!* After twenty-five years, I had become the person I had been longing for. I was finally living my life again. I was free!

After the operation, things were normal right away. I was ready to take on life. However, I was so happy to enjoy life free at last from all my hang-ups, I allowed fitness to fall by the wayside. I didn't realize how unfit and out of shape I was becoming as time ticked by. Now I could drink alcohol and eat chocolate when I liked without affecting my symptoms; I could go out and indulge while socializing. And so I spiraled out of control, lost in my new life without thinking about the consequences.

For a year and four months, I did nothing—and when I say nothing, I mean I did not exercise one bit. My body was out of shape. I had stiff joints to the point where I couldn't bend my knees without being in agony. All my years of occasional yoga and other exercise were wasted as I became so unfit and uncomfortable with myself. I felt lazy, with no energy or zest for life. My little boy suffered, because I didn't feel like doing much.

When I finally decided to get my lazy butt into gear, I heard about JNL Fusion through one of the moms at my son's school. She was a Zumba instructor who'd been teaching in our town for many years. I decided to try Zumba with a friend of mine, but it wasn't for me, as I am not really into dance-type workouts. I've always loved circuit classes, though, and Kerry Sanson (www.sansonfitness.com) told me about the JNL Fusion method. Kerry is a superb role model, and I am inspired by her endless dedication, drive, and enthusiasm. She also said that she was going to earn her master trainer certification at the JNL World Conference in Miami with none other than Jennifer Nicole Lee herself. I was so excited! I couldn't wait for Kerry to return so she could get the JNL Fusion method going here.

I was even more excited that Kerry would be the very first JNL master trainer in Wales.

I did my first JNL class on February 20, 2014, and have never looked back. I soon signed up to do a six-week fitness challenge with Kerry. It involved learning to eat healthfully by following a nutritional food diary and, most important, doing four JNL Fusion workouts a week. After just five JNL Fusion sessions over the course of only three weeks, I already felt stronger and more toned, and there were visible improvements. The aches and pains I had experienced because I had been inactive for nearly a year and a half were gone due to strengthening my body. When I started the challenge on March 1, I was forty-one years old. The scales calculated my body as being that of a thirty-six-year-old. On April 12, at the end of the challenge, I'd lost nine pounds and 4 percent body fat, and my body was now that of a twenty-six-year-old. I lost ten years in just six weeks! I've never felt my age, but knowing my body feels fifteen years younger than I am makes it even more worthwhile. I look and feel amazing, I have an unbelievable amount of energy, my skin feels softer and is glowing, and life just feels easier. I'm a JNL junkie! I've always enjoyed circuit training, and the JNL Fusion method is all that and more.

Oh, and one more phenomenal tip: after a hysterectomy comes menopause, and so do the hot flashes. I suffered tremendously with these until I started the JNL Fusion method and changed my diet. This leads me to say, "Hysterectomy—what hysterectomy? Hot flashes—what hot flashes?" I don't feel like I have any of these hang-ups because they are not part of my life anymore! As Jennifer says, "You have to push your body to change it."

Since my first JNL class, I have become a fan of Jennifer's and haven't stopped gathering as much information as possible to learn more ways to better myself. I've read her books (*The Fun Fit Foodie Cookbook* being a particular favorite), listen to her podcasts, follow her fitness guide, and more. I workout using Jennifer's DVDs a minimum of three times a week, and I also do one class a week with Kerry. I've never in my life felt inspiration like I get through the JNL Fusion method.

JNL Fusion is empowerment through mind, body, and soul, giving you so much strength in so many ways. Jennifer believes in you, so it's time for you to believe in you, too. I do!

Last but not least, here's one of Jennifer's quotes that inspires me the most: "It's time to put you back on your to-do list." My next goal: my own studio!

Connect with Carri-Anne Carmichael:
Facebook: Carri-Anne Smith Carmichael
Instagram / Facebook:
@jnlfusionjunky / JNLFusionJunky
@jennifer_nicole_lee_global / Jennifer Nicole Lee
Global @jennifernicoleleevip / Jennifernicoleleevip
For all your gym equipment needs:
Up & Running Fitness Services: One-off repair or on-going care
E-mail: Bruce Carmichael, gym equipment
technical specialist: bruce.c@live.co.uk
E-mail: Carri-Anne Carmichael, business partner and
administrator: carmichaelc@live.co.uk

CHAPTER FOUR

My Story
by Carolin Mildner

First, I want to thank Jennifer Nicole Lee for publishing my story in this amazing and incredibly inspirational book. It is a huge honor for me to share my journey to becoming the woman I am now.

In brief, my story is this: my life has changed completely over the past few years, thanks to losing almost eighty pounds and becoming the number-one JNL Fusion Master Trainer in Germany. I went from complete financial crash to strong-minded mom of two beautiful boys, from devoted but depressed wife to successful fitness expert and competitive athlete. But the full story requires much more than two sentences. Here we go.

I grew up in a small town in the mountains of Bavaria. My parents ran a Bavarian restaurant and hotel, so food was our livelihood. My mother always looked for fresh and healthful food for my little brother and me, but unhealthful options were always readily available. Our hotel was on the top of a mountain, and every day a little school bus took us to and from school. When I went on to higher classes (comparable to American high school), I attended a boarding school run by nuns. Our daily food was neither healthful nor tasty, and it wasn't always fresh, so we girls always kept tons of chocolate and sweets hidden away in our wardrobes. From this point I began struggling with my figure and weight.

I was always active, running half marathons, teaching skiing and snowboarding, and skiing in the mountains every weekend. My big love is horses, and from my teen years, I rode every day and trained horses for shows. Horseback riding is a complete body workout that requires a lot of strength, and all in all I trained very much—but my physique didn't change! I was very depressed and couldn't find a way out of the vicious cycle. That's when my bad journey of unhealthful and fad diets started. Sometimes I ate little to nothing, which was not very difficult at school, but then I ate everything in sight at home to make up for it. The yo-yo effect always got me in the end! My weight varied by fifteen pounds two or three times a year, and I ended up with two wardrobes—one for before the diet and one for after. I hated it. Sometimes I felt so disgusting and uncomfortable with my body that I didn't want to go out. This was very sad because I had always enjoyed life, having fun and laughing with friends. I was enslaved by my weight and figure—but I know I wasn't the only one. Many young women experience the same struggle, and if just one of them reads my story and changes her life, I've already won!

At fifteen I had a very bad riding accident in which my foot was completely separated from the joint. This began a long period of surgeries, hospital stays, and recovery. For almost a year and a half, I wasn't able to ride or do any other sports, and I drowned my sorrows in emotional eating. I gained about twenty pounds in this time, and though I lost it very quickly, I did it in a very unhealthful way. My metabolism was totally demolished, and even eating very small portions of salad and vegetables resulted in weight gain. Now my problems were twice what they had been before the accident.

I studied architecture, but I worked in the field only a short time because I wanted more from life than sitting in my office and drawing plans. I entered a phase of trying many jobs and had some hard experiences. Then I met my lovely husband, Andreas, a very professional and hardworking businessman and coach. He taught me about sales and doing big business, thus laying the foundation for my own consulting firm. I built and grew a very successful headhunting agency based in Munich.

Great times followed from there. My agency grew quickly, and I earned so much money that my life changed completely and my attitude greatly improved. I felt comfortable and successful. I traveled every week, went to lunch with clients who were CEOs of huge companies, and was known as a competent businesswoman. I learned that success is not all about money. The feeling of pride in reaching and achieving on your own makes you strong and sexy and helps your soul reach its potential. I had great pride in my company, and I worked very hard for its success. But I loved what I did, because it taught me what is possible when you leave your comfort zone. The key is to do things you've never done before, to push through your fears toward your goals. It took a lot of time, patience, and hard work to build my company, but it paid off, and it gave my family and me much success. Nothing is impossible if you pursue your dreams.

Even with hard work, it hasn't always been easy. The global economic crisis hit us hard, and I saw all of my blood, sweat, and tears go down the drain. All of the dedication, time, and energy I spent in building my business seemed to have been for nothing. I was in complete shambles, and we almost lost everything.

Long story short, I was done. I was very close to suffering from depression due to the financial crash. We had two children by this time, and I was home a lot with them. That's when the emotional and mindless eating started to happen. I was confused and sad, so I self-medicated with food—and lots of it! At that time I weighed about 170 pounds, and I was miserable. My entire body was sick, weak, and out of whack. I wasn't able to move properly—I was so riddled with stress that my body was all locked up. I was so out of shape that just climbing a flight of stairs left me breathless. I even had a hard time putting on my shoes because my big belly was in the way. My self-confidence went right out the door. I didn't feel sexy or pretty at all. I didn't even like to have my own husband see me naked. I was just so lost, scared, and lonely. I had to do something fast, as it was only going to get worse if I didn't.

I look back at this now and realize that it was the most difficult time of our lives. My husband was permanently on the road in order to earn money for us. I was left alone with my small children, fighting through the days to stay positive. My husband earned a decent salary, but sadly, the money would just flow right out through the holes in our company. I share this to let you know you are not alone in having personal hardships. There are no shortcuts and no excuses, but if you want it badly enough, you will achieve your weight-loss goals!

Naturally, this situation had an impact on our marriage. I had to find a solution. I was ready to make a positive change in my life. I was sad, tired, weak, and lonely. But I had to do something to regain control of my life, my body, my business, and my marriage—and of course to be the best mom I could be to my small children. So my search began. And as the saying goes, "When the student is ready, the teacher appears." When my children went to sleep, I searched online for information on diets, exercise, weight loss, and how to finally get in shape once and for all. And it happened—my aha moment. I came across Jennifer Nicole Lee.

Who was this? She had a history similar to mine, and she looked so amazing in the pictures—strong, sexy, powerful, successful, and desirable. Within a short time, I was a loyal follower and total JNL fan. I had a new and definite goal: to become fit and successful, just like Jennifer. I wanted to have her goddess body, her stunning "superhero" charisma, and her contagious positive energy.

I know that the saying "ask and you shall receive" is true, because I asked, and it happened! Thoughts became things. Through my desire to get out of my own dark rut, I found the solution and discovered that it is possible to have the life and body of your dreams. At that time I had no idea what else would come to pass: *Footsteps to Success,* our first book together! I not only got in shape, I became more successful and fulfilled.

After I got back on track, I began to really soak up the fitness information. I wanted to know and learn so much. I just had to find out how to crack the weight-loss code and how to train the right way for lasting results. I look back now and celebrate having trained with the JNL Fusion exercise videos, because I can see how they sparked my fitness fire. I kept myself motivated to stay on my weight-loss journey by reading every page of Jennifer's books, looking at her "before" and "after" photos, and purchasing her other fitness products and programs. I soaked up all the information like a sponge.

Losing weight, getting in shape, and gaining sleek, sexy muscle tone wasn't as hard as I thought it would be. I actually enjoyed it, and it was fun because I was following a successful fitness icon who *made* it fun, entertaining, and engaging. JNL wasn't boring or too serious, which made me want to work out more. I actually looked forward to training with her and doing the workouts. Little by little my body got stronger, fitter, and better. I actually started to crave healthful food. I also began to feel more attractive and beautiful. This was a fantastic feeling. For once, I loved the way I looked and felt. I wanted to take care of myself in order to fulfill my dream of having a firm, enviable body that made me feel sexy and desirable, as well as achieving lasting fitness and health. I was happy with myself, and I was happier with my husband and my kids. I just loved life so much. I was at my fullest potential and making the most of the once-horrible situation that the financial crisis had put me through.

I'm now an extremely busy entrepreneur. I love to work hard and focus on my business agendas and goals. I'm proud to say that I've worked very hard to create what I have. I'm blessed to be very happily married to my dream man. Andreas and I truly enjoy experiencing the wonder of nature every day as our two boys grow up quickly, right before our eyes.

My husband and I work a lot so our family can enjoy a certain type of lifestyle. My roles and responsibilities with our company are never-ending. On top of all that, I have to take care of my children, run a household, and look after the family dog. But I always schedule my workouts and eat right.

I finally got off my downward spiral and found my passion. I became a certified personal-fitness trainer and trained as an elite International Federation of Bodybuilding and Fitness athlete. Then I decided to really go for it and signed up for my first fitness competition. I even went another step by contacting Jennifer, who was hosting one of her world-famous one-day Fitness Model Factory mega-events. She was so excited about my story that she accepted me into her family and has since become my mentor. I have learned so much, my business has grown, and I'm proud to say that I am the top JNL Fusion Master Trainer in Germany.

I am incredibly grateful to Jennifer for this wonderful, unique, life-changing opportunity. I know it was my destiny to find these footsteps to success, because now I can share them with you all and pay it forward.

At this point I would like to thank my wonderful mentor. Jennifer, I thank you from the bottom of my heart. You motivated me in the most difficult times in my life. You gave me direction when I was so lost, and you showed me the footsteps to success and helped me to achieve my goals. You believed in me when I didn't believe in myself. As I followed in your successful footsteps, you gave me strength, discipline, and the necessary faith in myself. Without that belief, I never would have made it. You are forever my angel on earth. You have given me the greatest gift—faith in myself—and most important, my sister, you've taught me to never give up.

I still can't believe that I was once an overweight, depressed mom who had no clear vision of a promising future. And now, by following the footsteps to success, I am a professional fitness competitor. I still pinch myself, because my body transformation was so dramatic that I enjoyed huge success in my first professional competition season. In the spring of 2013, I even qualified for the German championship and placed in the top five in the professional circuit.

To sum it all up, I am the complete Cinderella story. I went from the bottom straight to the top! I never gave up; I kept the faith, believed in myself, and continued following the footsteps to success. I lost almost eighty pounds and I have kept it off, and now I enjoy being a fitness expert, coach, wellness consultant, and lifestyle expert in high demand. I'm even a published author. I was once a shy, overweight mom who hated her body, and now I love to model and rock the camera! I also love being a leader of the JNL Fusion method.

I'm so proud of my hard work and journey. I'm glad I was finally so determined to change my life that I found my mentor, Jennifer Nicole Lee, and have changed my life for good. My mission now is to pave the way for other moms and out-of-shape women. You can learn more in our book, *Footsteps to Success*. Here you will find everything you need to be supersuccessful, supersexy, and gain the amazing attitude you deserve.

In closing, I would like to encourage all women, especially mothers who are stressed and tired, to end the madness and start working out, eating healthfully, and taking care of you. You will become stronger for yourselves and for your families. And through your physical strength, you will become mentally, emotionally, and spiritually strong. With this type of empowerment, you will start to really love your life.

It *is* possible to live a life full of joy, fun, and love, the kind of life you've always dreamed about. But you have to start it. You need to summon the courage to get what you deserve in life, the fullness of happiness and love, of living as you want to and not as other people think you should. The hardest thing is that you have make the decision for yourself. You have to decide and then *act!*

We all have the same potential. I am not stronger or better than you; I just made the decision to take the first step and never go back. I'll never return to the overweight, overworked, and depressed woman I was, weak and afraid of the future, always expecting the worst, never having fun or joy. That is my past. But I love those hard times, because without them I would never have become the strong, sexy, and powerful woman I am today. Believe in your dreams, and love every situation you're in, because they form and design you. You *always* have the choice of your future. This is what I live for—this and my kids.

Believe in yourself! Always be yourself! Find out what you want in life, and then take it!

CHAPTER FIVE

Jesse Sink: Pushed to the Brink...and Beyond by Brandy Menefee

How 13,800 volts, two months in a coma,
and thirteen surgeries forced Jesse Sink
to find the strength not just to survive—but to thrive

Living the Dream

" At times I felt like the crazy kid in the family, the one who had these wild dreams."

Jesse Sink was nothing like his seven siblings. The middle child of an Indiana farming family, he fantasized about a world beyond his simple, conservative, constantly uprooted life. After moving eight times during his childhood and attending three different high schools, Jesse was determined to train hard, go full throttle, and make it big—to create a life that was the opposite of the one he knew.

This was an athlete who was so dedicated to his dream of becoming a successful fitness model that before he moved to New York to start booking jobs, he spent every day for four years giving his body the exact nutrition and exercise it needed to perform at its best. He treated his body with care and respect. Six short months after leaving Indiana against his parents' wishes to pursue a modeling career in New York City, twenty-one-year-old Jesse had already booked jobs for Calvin Klein and Tommy Hilfiger. He soon scored steady work with a catering company as a handsome hunk serving hors d'oeuvres to beautiful, successful, wealthy partygoers staring out penthouse windows that overlooked the big city. The country boy was living his dream.

Shocking

On the evening of December 2, 2006, Jesse had finished a catering gig and joined his colleagues for cocktails. As he ran to catch the last train out of Penn Station, he started to feel drugged. The six-foot-two-inch, two-hundred-pound athlete lost control of his vision and his speech. The last thing he remembered was standing inside Penn Station, staring at a monitor that was too blurry to read.

It was dark when Jesse woke up. He felt groggy. He opened his eyes and saw a metal platform in front of him. He turned to the side and saw the edge of a subway. He was lying facedown on top of a stopped train.

To steady himself and get down off the train, Jesse reached for a nearby rod with his right hand. That rod shot 13,800 volts through his body, frying him from the inside out, his blood boiling at 985 degrees. His shirt caught fire, flames shot from his shoulders and face, and he could hear his stomach cooking as he lay paralyzed by electric shock. He screamed until he lost his breath. He choked through the smoke and fire. He used his left hand to pull his fingers off the wire and fell eight feet onto the concrete platform.

"I could hear popping and crackling, which was my plastic backpack burning on my back," Jesse says. He grabbed the backpack, scorching his hand. Frantically he yanked off his shirt, and his skin started tearing off. He was charred. His right arm was numb. He could hardly hold up his head. He blacked out.

An unknown man appeared with a fire extinguisher to put Jesse out, called for an ambulance, and left to get help. The burning stopped, and Jesse regained consciousness. He'd been charbroiled and hosed with a fire extinguisher, but he didn't recall how or why. He didn't know what was wrong with him, but he knew it was bad. He needed to get help. Now.

In the distance he saw people walking for the next train. It was life or death, and there was no time to use an escalator. Jesse dropped down onto the train tracks and staggered across six tracks toward the platform with the people who would help.

Naturally right-handed, he extended his arm onto the platform to push himself up. His hand flopped onto the concrete and immediately flopped off. He had no feeling, no control of his hand. The clock was ticking as Jesse had to use his other arm to hoist himself up from the tracks before the next train hurtled up to the platform.

He finally emerged from the tracks, screaming, "Help me! Please help me!" The people screamed back. And fled. "I probably looked like a burnt zombie with plastic melting over me," he says. "A total walking nightmare."

Jesse's seared body stumbled and collapsed beside a concrete wall. He heard sirens in the distance as he struggled to stay awake. A team of EMTs sprinted toward him, and before they could finish setting up, Jesse flopped onto the stretcher. During the ambulance ride, he heard an EMT radioing the hospital: "Significant burns to a patient...we don't know if he's gonna make it."

With 60 percent of his upper body burned, doctors considered Jesse beyond repair. He was placed in a drug-induced coma and given two days to live. But his body fought to stay alive, and after forty-eight hours, a medical team began to operate. Midsurgery, Jesse felt the extreme heat from the medical lamp that hovered above his face. Then he fell back under sedation.

Jesse woke up, opened his eyes, and saw his sister standing at the edge of his bed. "Good to see you again! Do you know what today is?" she asked. Jesse, unable to speak, stared back at her. "It's February," she said. "You've been sleeping for two months."

He had no recollection of what he'd been through and no knowledge of the extent of his injuries. He just wanted the stabbing in his throat to stop. He discovered he had had a tracheotomy.

Jesse's body was exhausted from the trauma. Breathing was difficult. Blinking took all his energy. He'd lost fifty-seven pounds while in the coma. He had a horrible case of pneumonia from spending two months lying down. He could not move his neck, feet, or hands. It was five days before he mustered the strength to lift his head off the pillow.

Frustration and anger gave Jesse the energy he needed to turn his head to look and find out why he couldn't feel his right hand. He turned to his mother, who was weeping at his bedside.

"They cut my fucking arm off!"

"We didn't have a choice," she said. "We had to take your arm off. It was so burned." The decision had tortured her.

He had an elbow. The rest was gone. Jesse was officially an amputee.

The pain consumed him inside and out. Jesse could hardly move and barely breathe because his skin was so tight from multiple skin-grafting surgeries. It would take six years of stretching for the skin to mature. Six years. Not weeks—years. He describes it as "living inside an inner tube that's been sucked tight."

Nurses finally removed his body bandages. Jesse looked down at his chest and stomach. Staples held pieces of skin together. His torso was perforated and bumpy. Jesse was officially a burn victim. "You can lose an arm and get another arm," he says. "But you can't change the skin you were born with."

Discovering the severity of his burns and reality of his recovery was overwhelming. He could deal with losing his arm, but living as an amputee *and* a burn victim seemed unbearable.

Eventually, Jesse began to remember more details of the accident. One particular vision began to haunt him. But it wasn't a moment of pain from his electrocution. It was a moment of peace. Seconds after grabbing that subway rod, Jesse recalled having a vision of moving through a white tunnel and seeing two doves and a giant gate up ahead. Inside the tunnel, Jesse had been overcome with a calm feeling of peace, quiet, and love—"that feeling when you're out by a lake, sitting in a lawn chair, and the moon is out—times five." As Jesse moved closer to the gate, the white light at the end of the tunnel dissipated. He backed down the tunnel. And then the vision abruptly ended.

When he came to, he'd discovered his shirt burning, his back-pack melting, and his hand still clutching the rod wire that had just killed him with 13,800 volts. "That amount of electricity shuts your heart down," he explains, "but it's also enough voltage to restart it. Like a really strong defibrillator."

Now lying helpless in a hospital bed, Jesse was *pissed off*. Pissed he was still alive, pissed the hospital was keeping him alive, and pissed that God had let him live: "Why let me see the light and get me halfway home, and then take me away from that? What's the reason?"

Records show that Jesse had died a second time—his kidneys and pancreas shut down during his coma. Jesse had been considered code blue until doctors resuscitated him. *Why did I have to come back?* he wondered. *Why couldn't I have just stayed? Now I have to deal with all this pain. I've lost everything I have. Everything I've worked for. What do I have to live for now?*

Jesse couldn't talk, sit, stand, or walk. He'd have to learn how to do everything left-handed, but he didn't even have the strength to hold a piece of popcorn in his palm. He had no balance because his equilibrium was shot from lying flat for so long. His comfort relied on constant pain medication. His entire body was in agony. The medical bills were financially devastating. And there was no hope for his high-fashion and fitness-modeling career. He'd never fulfill his dream of appearing on the cover of *Men's Health*. The body he'd spent years working so hard to sculpt was ruined. His identity would never be the same.

The former athlete and model was now a 143-pound skeleton getting spoon-fed by his father, taking his first steps, and learning to write his name. *I'm twenty-one years old, and I feel like I'm in kindergarten,* he thought. *Who wants to live like this? I'm praying someone unplugs everything and I die.*

Doctors might have pieced him back together, but Jesse felt beyond repair. It was beyond depression. Jesse was suicidal. He gave up. He quit breathing. His face turned blue. A nurse tricked Jesse into taking a breath by pricking his toe with a needle. "Ah, see! Plenty of life!" she said. But he cried himself to sleep, begging God to not let him wake up: "There is absolutely no reason for me to open my eyes tomorrow."

Sink or Survive

There was probably one last thing that could kill Jesse Sink: moving back home to live with his parents. He returned in shame to the people and place he had been so determined to escape. "I've failed myself; I've failed my family," he told them. "I don't know why I'm here. Seriously, somebody please shoot me, *please.*"

Although Jesse assured his mother he would never harm himself, she wouldn't allow him to stay home alone. The parents who'd disapproved of Jesse's dreams now monitored his life 24-7. He dove into drugs and alcohol to escape, only to find himself in jail for thirty days after earning two DUIs within two months.

Behind bars, he could not escape. Every day he felt his parents intensely judging him, blaming his imprisonment and his current physical and mental condition on his lifestyle choices, and criticizing his drive to pursue his greatest aspirations. Jesse knew he was better than jail. But every day he was in there, it felt like his parents were winning. Every day they won. Every day he lost. Until one day he snapped. *I do not want them to win. I'm not going to let them win.*

He started focusing less on the tragedy and more on the triumph. Jesse fantasized. What if he had his arm back? What if health insurance could cover the cost of a prosthetic arm? What if he had a second chance? What could he do? What could he achieve? What could he prove to himself, his parents, and the world?

Jesse's electrocution had nearly sucked the life out of him. Twice. But the body Jesse had trained and treated so well refused to quit. It would not let 13,800 volts kill him. Instead of his arm blowing off and then him bleeding to death—a common fate of Penn Station graffiti artists who grabbed the same rod wire—Jesse's incredibly healthy body had been held together and insulated by muscle. The high voltage that should've killed him merely cooked him.

His body wouldn't let him give up. God wouldn't let him give up. Doctors wouldn't let him give up. The nurse who'd pricked his toe to trick him into breathing wouldn't let him give up. Jail wouldn't let him give up. Now it was Jesse's turn to not let himself give up. He had to push his mind the way he'd always pushed his body—beyond its limits.

Just as his body had rerouted his veins, Jesse now redirected his thoughts so they too could supply his heart with what it needed. Instead of giving up hope, he kept searching for it. He decided not to let his parents or his circumstances define him. Mentally shifting his focus and attitude allowed him to restrategize and change the blueprint of his life.

Three years after becoming an amputee, Jesse started using a custom-made bionic arm from Hanger Clinic, the nation's leading prosthetic provider. Without an arm, Jesse had been limited to working out his legs—squats and running—and strengthening one side of his frame, resulting in irregular body composition. But the Hanger prosthetic arm provided the limb control he needed and empowered Jesse to reach his full potential. He could now do push-ups, hold dumbbells, and bench-press up to 340 pounds. He could train others, carry groceries, and drive a car.

He spent the next three years using his Hanger arm to achieve a balanced body composition, allowing him to move and feel like the athlete he was born to be, and finally to compete publicly in bodybuilding and fitness competitions. He participated in a lifting contest sponsored by the United Powerlifting Association, squatting 610 pounds using his prosthetic arm.

Today Jesse Sink is a ProSupps-sponsored athlete, competitive body builder, private fitness trainer, nutrition coach, and inspirational/motivational speaker living in Los Angeles. He's an official spokesmodel for Manning Up USA, an organization for survivors to connect, share stories of triumph, and discuss how sports and fitness can be used to overcome adversity.

Jesse Sink is not like you and me. Not just because he survived 13,800 volts of electricity, two months in a coma, and thirteen surgeries. Or because he's died twice. Or because he's gone from being too weak to hold a piece of popcorn in his hand to being able to lift 610 pounds using a fake arm he straps on every day. Jesse Sink was unique long before he was electrocuted. By the age of twenty-one, his incredible discipline, drive, and dedication had forged him a massive muscular physique and a budding fitness-modeling career. "I trained until I had nothing left," he says. "I pushed myself beyond my limit every day, under as much weight as I could push."

And it's that same discipline, drive, and dedication that ultimately saved Jesse's life, pulling him through the darkest hours.

"There are a lot of people hurting," he says. "Everyone has pain. Everyone has a story. Strength is a state of mind. What you think holds you back can actually move you forward. The limits we have in life are only the ones we set for ourselves. What limits are you allowing to hold *you* back?"

Connect with Jesse Sink:
Instagram: @bionicjesse
Twitter: @jessesink
Facebook: jessesink
Fan Page: jessesink
E-mail: jasink85@gmail.com
Written by Brandy Menefee, ProStorytellers:
Instagram: @ProStorytellers
Twitter: @ProStorytellers
E-mail: brandy@ProStorytellers.com
Website: ProStorytellers.wordpress.com

CHAPTER SIX

A Journey of Healing
for a Special-Needs Mom
by Sheila Garcia

Looking at me today, you would be surprised to learn that this healthy, positive, vibrant special-needs mother-turned-author/ entrepreneur was once an overweight, sluggish, out-of-shape mom with little energy. Although I'd like to say my journey to physical and emotional healing was easy, it wasn't. You are probably wondering how I did it. How was I able to go from such an unhealthy place to coming out on top? I lost weight and got fit. I look and feel better than I ever have, and best of all, I have risen above it to become the best mom I can be, all while feeling happy and spirited. I am sure you'd like to know the secrets. Who doesn't want to be inspired by a transformation story?

There are a lot of special-needs moms who feel like they have lost their sense of self. Who have become emotionally drawn to comfort food. Who are exhausted from the everyday to-do list that has taken over their lives. Who have no energy to exercise or provide self-care. Think about your own life, whether you're a special-needs mom or not. Have you ever felt like you lost control? If you did, how did you turn that around?

My journey to self-healing began first by believing. I had a passionate desire to change so I could live a happy life and feel good both inside and out. I did this by believing in myself, never giving up, and staying on course with my goals.

This is how my story begins.

In March 2002, I gave birth to a beautiful and healthy baby boy. I had waited a long time for him to come into my world, so you can only imagine the joy I felt that day. When the time came to bring him home, I remember being wheeled out of the hospital with our son dressed in a soft blue cotton outfit etched with choo-choo trains, and covered in a heavy yellow blanket. My husband followed us, pulling a big red wagon full of unopened gifts. Although spring was right around the corner, the air was cold that March day, the clouds were a shade of gray, and snowflakes were starting to fall softly from the sky.

The ride home was quiet, as we didn't want to startle our son, who was sleeping peacefully in his car seat. As we pulled up in front of our house, I whispered into his ear, "We are home, baby." I was so ecstatic to finally arrive home with our bundle of joy that I took him right to his new nursery, which was filled with plush animals, books, toys, and rattles galore. I sat in the rocking chair next to his crib, looking at the pale yellow wall stenciled with bumblebees flying to their hive, and love gleamed through my eyes as I held my son in my arms. Slowly I sat up from the rocking chair, reached into his crib, and took out a musical pillow that played Brahms's "Lullaby." I rocked back and forth, staring down at him, this miracle we'd created, stroking his soft pink face and touching his little fingers, and I thought how blessed we were.

Night finally arrived, and it was time to put him in his white lace bassinet next to our bed. My eyes were starting to get heavy from days in the hospital without sleep, but the only thing I feared was not hearing him if he cried in the middle of the night.

The first couple of years were precious times I will cherish always. But during that time, I also noticed my son wasn't meeting one of the milestones of speech. We assumed it was because he was a shy little boy, but we decided to have him evaluated.

In April 2004, our lives changed forever. At the age of two, my son was diagnosed with PDD-NOS, which stands for pervasive developmental disorder—not otherwise specified, and is under the umbrella of autism spectrum disorder. Children with this diagnosis have difficulty with communication, social interactions, and behaviors. When the neurodevelopmental pediatrician gave us this diagnosis, I felt helpless, uncertain, and fearful for his future—our future. You can only imagine my devastation. I left the doctor's office that day with a list of resources to call, but with little hope. I felt as though the doctor had given me a script sending us to a different country where I didn't know the language or culture. Little did I know that day was the beginning of the journey that has shaped me into the positive and strong woman I am today.

The day after receiving my son's diagnosis, my fear grew. My dreams and goals for him seemed to have been lost in an instant. It immediately became paramount for me to move and push myself to help him, just as most mothers would do. When he was born, I couldn't wait for him to start talking, and hear him say his first recognizable word. What would it be? Would it be *mama, dada, baba?* I couldn't wait to have that back-and-forth conversation with him where he would point and ask a million times, "What's that?" as most babies and toddlers do. I knew there had to be a sweet voice inside this beautiful boy, and I was determined to get him to therapy right away so he could begin to progress toward this and other important milestones.

In the midst of navigating the uncharted territory of our son's autism diagnosis, I neglected my health because of my all-consuming pursuit of the best care for him. The way I dealt with the emotional pain was by burying myself in researching therapies, alternative treatments, and numerous special programs. When I wasn't doing this, I was busy running my son back and forth to therapy, school, and doctor appointments. I had gained an astounding sixty pounds during my pregnancy, and even though I desperately wanted to lose the weight, I struggled with eating healthfully, finding time to exercise, and taking moments to care for myself. As a result, I often found comfort in convenience foods, especially when I was on the go with my son. My weight would constantly yo-yo, and I couldn't seem to maintain my desired body image. I had borderline-high cholesterol levels and body aches and pains. I felt weak and stressed out by the demands of my everyday to-do list—which, by the way, did not include any time for me. Years of nonstop worry and fear about my son's future started to take a toll on my physical and emotional well-being. I was exhausted and depleted. This was the pivotal moment for me, and I clearly remember sitting on my couch, thinking I couldn't continue on this path another day.

I am sure that all mothers, especially special-needs ones, can relate to the natural tendency to put your needs second to those of your child. And there is a rise in the number of mothers raising special-needs children today. It is only natural to put yourself on the back burner when you are caring for a child with a disability. Although that care is rewarding, it can become stressful due to the unexpected calls from school, medical emergencies, and new behaviors that may arise. Sometimes you just feel like you're on a runaway roller coaster that never ends. And just as I learned, if you continue to put your needs last over the long term, the outcome may be exhaustion, depression, irritability, and other ailments. Then there are the other issues of dealing with isolation and challenges with personal relationships. Your needs can often be overlooked. But when your needs are taken care of, it can translate into a positive energy that will benefit not only you, but also the whole family.

At the age of thirty-eight, I knew I was headed in a downward spiral; if I stayed on that path, it would be detrimental to my health, and worse, it could possibly affect my ability to take care of my family. I decided to stop making excuses and turn my struggles into triumphs. In January 2012, my restart moment began when I decided, once and for all, to reclaim my health. This was not a New Year's resolution but instead an evolution. I took the power of that new-year momentum and made some deliberate and specific changes. I decided to become more active, pay attention to my eating habits, and care for my mind and spirit. I knew that in order to succeed, I had to have spiritual strength and tenacity.

As part of my journey of healing, I made a commitment to myself to become more active. I hired a personal trainer to come to my home and work with me on an exercise regimen twice a week. I knew I needed someone to hold me accountable and kick my butt into gear! My trainer introduced me to a method that really shaped my body and mind: the JNL Fusion method. Doing short, intense, interval circuit training worked for getting me back into shape, tight and toned, and fueled with the ability to lose more weight. Finding an exercise program that you love keeps you more motivated to get up and work out, particularly when so many other things are begging for your attention. Of course there were days that I felt unmotivated to continue with my exercise routine and eating healthfully, but in those moments I reminded myself of my purpose. With my purpose firmly in place, I knew it was important for me to move forward. After a couple of weeks of doing this method, I noticed an overall increase in my energy levels, endurance, and stamina. Doing this type of exercise, incorporating healthful eating habits by cooking at home, and supplementing with vitamins made a huge difference in my overall health and well-being.

Fast-forward to today. I start each day by training in the privacy of my home, doing the JNL method along with other types of exercise routines five to six times a week. Being innovative with my exercise regimen is really rewarding to me. Because I am consistent and dedicated, I am able to maintain a healthy weight and feel good both inside and out.

During my journey of healing, I experienced a painful time in which I discovered my deepest truth: I had spent years punishing myself for my son's diagnosis. I hadn't made my well-being a priority, because I felt I wasn't worthy or deserving of it. Not only was I hurting myself, essentially I was hurting my son. He was missing out on building a healthy and positive relationship with me because I was too busy blaming myself. As a mother, I want my son to see me as a positive role model, and to know the importance of taking care of your well-being. Furthermore, I wanted to start feeling healthy so he could see the happy, spirited person I truly am. Through the process of my self-healing journey, and by making this important realization about how I was sabotaging my own wellness, my relationship with my son only deepened, and our bond grew stronger.

To keep my self-healing going, in the summer of 2012, I decided to submit my application to the JNL Fitness Model Factory. With much surprise, I learned I was one of many women selected to attend and meet my fitness mentor, Jennifer Nicole Lee. I had the pleasure to meet and work with someone I admire in the fitness industry and many other women who were chosen to be a part of this event. In order to stay propelled through my transformation, I continued to follow Jennifer and other fitness enthusiasts on social media sites, and read motivational quotes and inspirational articles and books. One thing Jennifer says a lot is "Believe that you can and you will." That word "believe" has such a powerful meaning, and it has influenced my life in a positive way. When I made the decision to believe that I deserved a happy and healthy life, instead of blaming myself for my son's diagnosis and punishing myself with unhealthy behaviors, I was able to fully commit to my journey. The word "believe" always resonated with my soul and pushed me to continue on my journey toward healing.

While I was on this path of soul-searching, I developed an affinity for fitness and nutrition. With previous experience in a wellness practice, I realized the avenue of fitness and health coaching was right for me. When I discovered this, I became aligned with my true passion. I decided to get my certification as a personal trainer, JNL Fusion trainer, and holistic health coach. My studies as a fitness coach and in the area of integrative nutrition have really shaped and empowered me to be the woman that I am today. With this experience and guidance, I was inspired to launch my business, Sheila Fitness ~N~ Healthy Lifestyle, through which I educate, support, and coach other women who are struggling with weight issues to get back into shape so they can feel and look great. It is a passion of mine to empower women to take time to refresh, revitalize, and care for themselves. After all, we deserve it, right?

My transformation has made a significant impact on my life. Not only did I fall in love with fitness, I also learned what foods fuel my body. Every morning, I start with either a smoothie or fresh juice, which gives me a boost of energy to start my day out right. This has completely shifted the way I eat to stay healthy. Finding my way back into the kitchen was another step I took to live the life I desire. I regained my culinary skills to create healthful meals for my family to enjoy. I filled a void by cooking at home, which has made a huge difference in my health and my family's health, because I am able to control what ingredients go into our meals, as well as our portion size. I believe that finding your true passion contributes to a healthy lifestyle. This experience has empowered me to author my first cookbook, *Healthy Cooking in a Pinch.*

During this process, I blossomed and gained confidence to accomplish things that I once thought were impossible. I turned the word "can't" into "can," and "impossible" into "possible." This courage and bravery are characteristics I adopted from my son. His continued efforts to cultivate success in the areas of speech, socialization, and learning have taught me to never give up. He has made leaps and bounds in the past two years by placing one brick on top of the other. Through him I have learned that sometimes it may take baby steps, but eventually you will get there. I have faith now to continue on this healing journey, and I know my son will flourish along the way.

Franklin Delano Roosevelt famously said, "The only thing we have to fear is fear itself." When faced with adversity, you have a choice to fall into self-pity and wallow in fear, or to bounce back by turning your life around and becoming strong, healthy, and positive. Although it took me years, I chose the latter. Getting to where I am today required a daily commitment to consciously affirm within myself that I was worthy of my goals, and that I could accomplish them. It required continual reinforcement until I grew to believe in my heart that I deserved the healthy and abundant life I wanted. Just like a butterfly trying to emerge from its cocoon, you have to go through struggles to be able to use your wings to fly. It is never too late to live the life you desire and deserve.

As you can see from my own story, it pays to believe in who you are and to know you have the power within you to create the life you want. Remember to say to yourself every day, "It's possible," and keep going until you find your inner truth. Be patient and kind to yourself, and give yourself permission to be joyous, healthy, and happy.

Sheila Royce Garcia is founder and owner of Sheila Fitness ~N~ Healthy Lifestyle. She is an author, personal trainer, JNL Fusion instructor, and holistic health coach. Her mission and passion is to coach women who are struggling with weight issues and unhealthy eating habits to become more active and develop healthier food choices. Her biggest achievement to date is authoring her first cookbook, Healthy Cooking in a Pinch: A Family Cookbook on How to Create Healthy Meals on Busy Days.

For more information, please visit
www.SheilaFitnessNHealthyLifestyle.com, www.
HealthyCookinginaPinch.com, www.facebook.
com/SheilaFitnessNHealthyLifestyle.

CHAPTER SEVEN

From Victim to Warrior
by Christine Jackson

My personal journey started what seems like yesterday and yet an eternity ago at the same time. But the length of time is of no consequence; it is all the moments within that matter. The ups and downs, the battles, and the victories great and small—they are all worthy of celebration, for they are what made me who I am today.

I had been overweight a majority of my life since childhood. I constantly struggled, and yo-yo dieting was killing my mind, body, and spirit. In 2004, I had the miracle of my first and only child. At four feet, ten inches tall, I was still very overweight and working to get down to 180 pounds. It seemed like that was as good as it was going to get, and I accepted this. I was satisfied. I had my child; I needed nothing else.

In early 2006, my world fell apart: *"Your child has autism."* These words sent me spiraling down to a dark and dangerous place. I focused only on my son, sacrificing myself in the process. I felt unworthy of any focus or attention. How could I be? The only thing that mattered was my child. All of my time, my attention, every waking moment, even my sleep—it was all consumed with *How did this happen? Why did this happen? How can I fix this?*

As Devin progressed, my health and well-being declined. In 2011, I hit rock bottom. My weight was at an all-time high of 340 pounds. I was morbidly obese. I could not walk. I had to use a wheelchair or a walker. I was completely dependent on others to go anywhere. At forty years old, I had the declining health of someone well into their sixties. My obesity had led to a multitude of health issues. To this day I have no cartilage left in either knee. My health was so poor that I was at risk of losing my job. I could not take care of my son. I had failed. I had failed at protecting my child and helping him progress. I had failed at earning a living to support him and myself. I was put on medical disability and faced the possibility of being permanently disabled.

Being on disability required me to go back and forth to a multitude of medical appointments, and the doctors issued many dire warnings: "You are a time bomb." "You must lose weight or you *will die*." "You are morbidly obese. There is nothing we can do for your knees." I was on medication for blood pressure, diabetes, fatty liver, high cholesterol, and irregular heart rhythm.

My aha moment finally came one evening when I had Devin curled up on my lap. I looked down at this angel and thought, *How can I say I love him if I am willing to die and leave him on this earth without me?* The next morning I began researching different clinics and programs. I did not want to do surgery. I wanted to do this the right way, once and for all. I found the best program I could. Nutritionally sound, no quick fixes—just old-fashioned hard work! I had to lose sixty pounds to even become mobile enough to exercise. Through the process, I had ups, I had downs. I had times when I wanted to give up and give in. I wanted results quickly, and if I plateaued, I wanted to just stop. But for every moment I breathed easier, for every moment out of my wheelchair, for every moment I could take a step holding my son's hand, that small voice in my head kicked in: *Don't give up, your miracle is coming. Don't give up, Devin needs you.* I was determined to be my own hero. Be my own cheerleader. I was determined to go from victim to warrior.

The hardest thing I had to combat was the feeling that I was being selfish. I feared I was not worthy and was a bad mother to divert any time, attention, or money away from Devin and invest in myself. Well, that guilt was the devil speaking, and the devil is a liar! Investing in myself and my health was the very thing Devin needed his mother to do. It was a courageous act to step out in faith and do what I had to do in order to be a better mother to my child.

Within a year I was off all medications. I began to train harder. Again, there were times I didn't see results quickly enough, and I had people, even trainers, tell me this was as good as it was going to get. "You are never going to be a fitness model." "You are too old to progress past this point." I was ready to accept this. Then one day I was researching the best exercises for shedding and toning, and I came across this woman's page. She was the most gorgeous woman I had ever seen, and she had the most perfect physique—toned, fit, healthy, and strong. And there was something different. Something unique about her photos that made them unlike any others I had seen. There was a fire within her that exuded from her photos. She was a true powerhouse.

Well, I researched her a little further. I found out her name was Jennifer Nicole Lee, a fitness model, trainer, and cookbook writer. OK, nice. Then I read her story. I saw her "before" and "after" photos, and I saw she was a mom. My second aha moment! She was *real! She knows the struggle,* I thought. *And oh my God—she went from overweight to fitness model! If she can do this,* I *can do this!* So I began to follow Jennifer. She was my inspiration to take it all the way. I had now transformed from "OK, I just want to walk" to "I am going to *kick some trash!"* My entire mind-set changed. I was empowered! I trained harder, ate cleaner, and stayed on course. I kept quoting *my she-ro* in my mind. *Never give up, never give in, train to* win!

My life's dream was to meet this woman. Somehow I knew that I would, because God is good, and thoughts become things! In April 2014, I was at the Europa Games Get Fit and Sports Expo when my girlfriend started shaking me, saying, "Oh my God, Christine, isn't that your girl?" I said, "What? Who?" I looked and there she was— my she-ro! I ran to Jennifer, jumping up and down like I had won the lottery. I could not believe it! No surprise to me, she was exactly the powerhouse I envisioned—just as real and as genuine as I had perceived her to be. At that moment, my internal flame kicked into high gear. We began communicating; I did a podcast with her, and now this chapter. I learned we share the same vision. We want people to know you absolutely can take back control of your life. You absolutely can defeat all odds. You absolutely can reinvent yourself at any age. It is not your circumstances that matter but your will to go from victim to warrior to champion to mentor.

Since meeting Jennifer, I now train four times a week. I am down to 160 pounds and still going. Two months ago I ran my very first 5K—with no cartilage. I train to overcome, to finish and finish *strong*. I am not satisfied with simply being a smaller version of my former self. I am strong! I run, and jump, and play with my son. I can take him wherever I want by myself. I no longer need a wheelchair or a walker. To the orthopedic doctors who said I would never walk, never wear anything other than sneakers, I invite you to come dancing with me while I'm wearing my heels. I invite you to my next 5K. I invite you to do CrossFit, boot camp, and JNL Fusion training with me. Why? Because I can do it! I never gave up, I never gave in, and I am training to *win*. Be your own hero! Whatever your journey is, it starts in your mind. Nothing is more powerful than the human soul on fire.

CHAPTER EIGHT

Jackie's Story
by Jackie Zuene

The hardest part of writing this story was deciding where to begin on this incredible journey of my life. I wanted to be able to really take my reader through the powerful, extraordinary, and lifesaving experience that led me to create Mind Body Fitness Solutions, a lifestyle-counseling service. My business is the result of changing my life and the life of my son's mother forever.

I have a nine-year-old son named Garret. At conception, he was one of three babies in my womb. Sadly, Garret was the only child to survive my pregnancy. And any child God allows to survive such tragedy deserves the best mother in the world. So this is my story, written for all to see. It is the story of my emotional and physical fight back to life so that I could give my only son a healthy, sober, loving, considerate, honest, grateful, and incredibly humble mother—the mom he deserves.

In January 2010, at 6:27 p.m., I received a phone call from my stepmother, telling me that my father was very ill and had been rushed to the hospital. I immediately called the hospital to get whatever information I could. To my surprise, the news was very bad. The nurse told me my father would not live through the night.

I reside in Columbus, Ohio, and my father lived in Parkersburg, West Virginia. The travel time was close to two hours. I had no time to lose.

Dad and I

My father was more than a parent, he was my friend. I have heard many say he was also one of my biggest enablers. Whatever the case, my father and I were very close. From the time I was twenty-two years old, we would speak on the phone every morning at five thirty, and we talked for at least an hour. The news of his sudden impending death was earth-shattering.

I packed a bag and called all the family members, as well as a dear friend of twenty-five years named Bernard Grigsby, who was like a member of our family. Bernie lived in Clarksburg, West Virginia, and he immediately traveled to Parkersburg to meet us. It was a long, sleepless night of worry, with family members arriving from Ohio, Maryland, and other parts of West Virginia to say good-bye to my father. The night was touch and go. My father was on breathing machines and never awoke. As we all braced ourselves for the worst, he just held on. We stayed through the night, awaiting the agony before us.

The following morning, Bernie and I decided to have a picnic in the intensive care waiting room. We hadn't seen each other in close to a year, and we used that time to catch up. Bernie went to Kroger and bought a cooler, lunch meat, Pringles, and some nuts. We sat in the hospital together, catching up on each other's lives and reminiscing about old times.

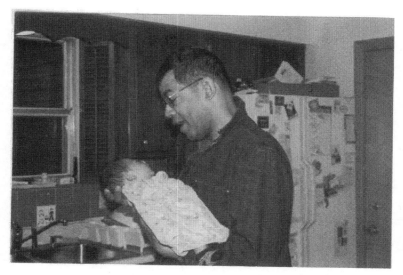

Bernie holding Garret at three days old

Later that day, we were advised that my father was out of immediate danger. The following day was a workday, and Bernie and I both had work obligations. We decided to go home and return to the hospital later in the week. We went to the gas station, where he insisted on filling up my car. We had spent an incredible day together. We were like two kindred spirits. Bernie and I had shared a long friendship, and he had always been there when I needed a friend or even a surrogate father if mine was busy.

I went to my training class the next day and turned off my cell phone for the morning session. I turned it back on at ten o'clock to check my voice mail, and there were several frantic messages from my sister, telling me to call her right away. I returned her call immediately and received the absolute shock of my life. Bernie had been found unconscious on his bathroom floor. I was frantic. I rushed home, packed a bag, and drove to Ruby Memorial Hospital in Morgantown, West Virginia, to offer Bernie whatever moral support he needed.

While driving those three hours to Bernie's bedside, I had time to think about the prior few years. They had been horrible. I had survived the demise of my marriage to a man I'd loved more than life. I had survived a horrible relationship with an abusive alcoholic who'd stolen many of my belongings and much of my money. It was the moral support of my lifelong friend Bernie that had gotten me through it. This was my chance to repay him for being there those past three years of trauma and abuse.

When I arrived at the hospital, my brother Mike met me in the lobby. Mike had wanted to be at Bernie's side because Bernie was like family to all of us. It also happened to be Mike's birthday that day. As we walked the hall to Bernie's room, Mike gave me the news. My friend Bernie was dead. He'd died on his bathroom floor, alone. His sister had elected to donate many of his organs, so he was being kept on life support for the moment. He'd had a massive brain bleed and was gone.

Just like that, my life began to plunge into darkness. I walked into the room and saw Bernie lying there, attached to the very machines he and I had seen keeping my father alive less than twenty-four hours before. But my father was alive, and Bernie was dead. I stayed in the room with his body for two days, alone, while they found recipients for his organs. It was hell. I was in a state of total shock. I mourned him so severely that I began to drink heavily.

Meanwhile, my father was still very ill. I spent the next three months traveling to three different hospitals trying to save him. My brother had him moved to Charleston so that he could get advanced care. But slowly and horribly he deteriorated, and finally he died. It took almost four months.

I didn't understand how God could have taken both of my fathers from me. I began a downward spiral into alcohol, prescription drug abuse, and overeating. I gained seventy pounds. I collapsed at work because my health was so poor. I had to be rushed to the hospital.

One day after being released from the hospital, I was sitting home alone, watching a show on the WE network called *Secret Lives of Women*. It featured a lady I'd never heard of, a woman by the name of Jennifer Nicole Lee. As I watched the show, tears began to stream down my face. I was beside myself with emotion at the vast change she'd made in her own life by just deciding to do it. I was so overcome by her success in achieving her goal of lifetime fitness, along with mental and physical health, that I cried for two days.

During that time, a friend and personal trainer I know well, Gary Martin, came to visit me. I told him Jennifer's story and about how watching the show inspired me to want a new, healthy life. Gary was equally moved by the immediate change Jennifer's special had had on my life, and he was eager to help me reach my goals. He went to the Arnold Classic, a body-building competition, that year, and Jennifer Nicole Lee was there, signing autographs and changing lives. He stood in line for her on my behalf and got an autographed photo of her for me. When he gave it to me, I could not stop crying. I was so moved, I immediately embarked on the life changes Jennifer promoted. I dropped seventy pounds and started a business to change lives, with Jennifer as my silent angel. One day four years later, I got mad at Gary and tore up the autographed photo to hurt him, but I immediately regretted it. When I finally told him about it, he reached out to Jennifer again via e-mail, requesting a new signed photo for me. To his surprise and my total shock, a package came to my home with a new autographed photo. I totally lost it—I cried for a day and a half. I was overwhelmed to know that there was someone out there as incredible and gracious as Jennifer Nicole Lee, and that I had the added bonus of a best friend who was a personal trainer as well as someone who really understood how to move me. I am again on fire, via Jennifer Nicole Lee, for myself and for every other woman out there who thinks it can't be done. It can.

Jennifer's influence led me to a breakthrough in all areas of physical and mental well-being. With Jennifer as a constant, silent inspiration and role model, I found my way back to a fit, healthy life. She helped train me to live healthy all over again. She continues to help me tap into my own physical strength daily.

I now live life to the fullest with and for my son. I joined with Gary Martin, the man who was my physical proxy for Jennifer and who taught me to retrain my body and fight for my life, in a business venture. We decided to combine our areas of expertise and form Mind Body Fitness Solutions. Now I have the opportunity to change and save lives, just like my idol for life, Jennifer Nicole Lee. I want to give the world the freedom I now live for—freedom through mental and physical health.

CHAPTER NINE

What Doesn't Challenge You Doesn't Change You by Tonya Mecum

They say beauty is wasted on the young. Is that so? In my twenties, I felt like I could and would rule the world. I finished college in the '90s and spent a year living in San Luis Obispo, California, looking for direction. I decided to move to Cupertino, the heart of Silicon Valley, where exciting things were happening. I was surrounded by major corporate offices, and names like Sony, Toshiba, IBM, Xerox, Netscape, and Sun Microsystems seemed to light up the sky. I was from a small town where agriculture and education were the main sources of employment. Now I felt as though I had so many opportunities to learn; I had stepped into an exciting new world.

I had always maintained an active life. Whether it was soccer, dancing, basketball, or cheerleading, I was always involved in some kind of physical activity. But I had never learned to eat properly. I was a latchkey kid whose babysitter was often a large bag of Doritos and my favorite episode of *Three's Company, Wonder Woman,* or *Fantasy Island,* or my videotape of *Grease.* I often went to a friend's house before basketball practice, and our group of eleven girls would devour anything the host family made available to us. I was raised on meals from a family-friendly fast-food restaurant that was available in every city we drove through. For years, my family even gave me gift certificates to that restaurant (which shall remain unnamed) so that I could have my favorite lunch at will.

JENNIFER NICOLE LEE

As a college graduate with a new lease on life, I was making my own money, living in a big city, and going to San Francisco often enough to justify driving an automatic car. I was building my resume; in 2000, I finally got a job with an industry-leading software company. I had determination and drive, and I knew I was going to make something of myself in this company, building a legacy of success. I had just moved in with a coworker and had been dating some extremely attractive men. I had a cute car and a cute little attitude to go with it, just like my hot girlfriends did. We hit the clubs, danced all night, drank fruity cocktails, and had new outfits every weekend. Oh, the memories! The world was my oyster—new place to live, new job that I loved—and I was moving up the corporate ladder at the software company, even without any technical background.

Then I met the boyfriend who spoiled my joy by throwing an adult-size tantrum every time I went on a business trip. When I lost my heart, I lost my soul for a little while—and immediately lost twenty pounds, too. I felt good about being skinny simply because I was starting to get noticed again. My boyfriend made sure I emptied my closet of all items that were even slightly revealing or sexy, which provided me an opportunity to fatten up a bit. The intimacy had left. I began traveling every four to six weeks, which was tearing the relationship apart, but I had a corporate card and was impressing clients with fancy dinners of exotic foods and wine. My trips often lasted three days, during which time 100 percent of my meals seemed out of my control. I put all of my energy into my work, but my poor attitude was blocking me from bringing in the contracts. I was the difficult yet detail-oriented business development manager who was all business during the day and then treated my clients like royalty at night by shoving rich foods and desserts down their throats.

Needless to say, I was no longer getting eight hours of sleep, and I spent my time working instead of working out. My diet was rich in saturated fats, sugar, red meat, processed airplane food, drive-throughs, and ice cream. I was torturing my body. I noticed that

68

I was having a harder time making my way down the aisle of the airplane. I felt my body forcing my luggage to bump the seats as I passed by.

My physical insecurities started to greatly affect my negotiation skills. My lack of confidence was also creating a negative outlook on life. I was displeased with my job; I was still heartbroken and drowning my sorrows further with food and wine. By now I was in therapy. My doctor prescribed me Xanax and Ambien. My left eye had a nonstop twitch. I was bursting at the seams, physically and mentally. I thought if I moved to a new town, started a new life, my outlook would change or my stress level would diminish. So I made a huge change and moved to Colorado to begin transitioning from software sales to fitness.

Fitness was something I had dreamed about as a child. I wanted to have the shapely legs and tiny waistlines I saw on TV in the 1980s. I watched Gilad's *Bodies in Motion*, the twenty-minute workout with the sexy ladies in their unitards, leg warmers, and big hair, and I stayed glued to the TV when *Solid Gold* was on. At thirteen I convinced my mom to join the gym with me, and I recall walking by the front desk and stating out loud that someday I would own a gym so I could help others get healthy and feel confident.

As I settled into life in Colorado, my plans started to move ahead. I began researching videos online as I prepared to become a certified personal trainer. I came across a video of a gorgeous woman with muscles *and* shape, who had an energy and presence that spoke to me. She was motivating and real. She was beautiful and spunky. She was Jennifer Nicole Lee, fitness celebrity. I borrowed some new cardioblasting moves from her to throw my clients off, and I used her high-intensity interval training workout style to build my Tabata classes. Then I discovered that there was a full program called JNL Fusion, and I could become certified! I was thrilled. But I was also broke. I hadn't planned on a new lifestyle when I quit my lucrative career for a happy life. I didn't think the two could go together.

I waited an entire year to apply for the JNL World Con, with the understanding that I was committing to myself and a healthier body to represent my business. I concentrated on my workouts. I didn't eat as many bags of Doritos. I attended the 2014 World Con…and felt completely out of place.

As I arrived at the registration desk, I was shocked to see Jennifer greeting every woman as we signed in. The executive staff checked us all in and verified our information. I have been to countless conferences that felt like a cattle call of guys in suits and gals in heels, walking and talking swiftly on their cell phones without acknowledging my presence. I was used to not being noticed anymore. I was comfortable in the background and had mastered the art of becoming invisible when necessary. But Jennifer was not going to let me hide. She wrapped her arms around me and held me tight, giving me a wonderful compliment the moment we met. She led me to the conference room, where I found her tanks, posters, books, sweats, hats, and videos. I loved the motto "strong is the new skinny," and I saw how tiny the tanks were. I looked up and realized that every single woman in the room was gorgeous. I mean *gorgeous*! And every woman was smiling. Every woman wore a tight dress to accentuate every curve that had clearly been worked hard. But me, I had a maxidress that was made to cover my curves.

I attended the JNL World Con alone but had the fortune to room with an amazing woman from the United Kingdom who had two adorable girls and a loving, doting husband. She immediately made me feel welcome and that I had a friend throughout the event.

Initially I wanted to do my own thing so I could absorb as much information as possible and not be influenced by anyone around me. From the first moments of this wonderful experience, I had planned on distancing myself. But why? Why was I so fearful? Why was I so lonely? Why was I here?

I grew emotionally during the seventy-two hours I spent in Miami. I listened intently to what the amazing Jennifer Nicole Lee had to teach me. I was immediately impressed with the level of experience and many accolades the JNL Fusion team possessed. I learned more about proper form and technique than at any other seminar I had attended. I watched Jennifer interact with the attendees and her staff. Jennifer was *real*. She knew everything about everyone, everything that was being presented by her staff, and the backstory for every JNL Fusion enthusiast in the room. She knew how each piece of equipment worked and could have easily stepped in for any of her support staff if needed. My respect for Jennifer grew exponentially. I became overwhelmed with a feeling of belonging, one I had not felt in some time. Something clicked. After rubbing elbows with other beautiful, empowered women who believed in me the same way I believed in them, I was a new woman. Where had these women been all my life?

I got the nerve to go up on stage to lead some of the moves during a workout. I thought I was going to pass out! I always give 100 percent, but being on stage in front of these amazing women made me try even harder. Jennifer's photographer, Rula, snapped a shot of me doing the Heisman jump, my tank loosely bouncing around, my chubby cheeks bright red under my hat, my knees high as I forced them into the appropriate position, and my flabby arms pumping. Damn. At the time I'd thought I was working hard and showing the room what I had! But after seeing the photos a few weeks later, all I could think was *Now everyone can see me in action. What sort of representative am I of my own business and now of JNL Fusion?* I had to make a change. I had to get serious.

Jennifer led us through multiple mental exercises to calm our inner voices. We meditated. We enjoyed an hour of yoga together. Several other ladies shared their stories about how JNL Fusion had changed their lives. I was truly touched and moved by every single story. That was when it hit me: I wanted to be up there sharing my story in 2015. I *needed* to be on stage sharing my story. I *was going* to be on stage sharing my story!

My story has to have a happy ending. I only expect a happy ending. I know I am capable of making my own future. I have the tools. I have been successful before, and I can be successful again.

This is a new chapter in my life, and forty is just around the corner. It's time for me to feel good again. I decided to break free of the negative self-talk and let go of the memories of negative criticism so I can allow myself to receive the wonderful things I know I have coming to me.

From January 21 through June 15, 2014, I lost eight pounds, 7 percent body fat, and three pants sizes. I zeroed in on my nutrition and used my JNL Fusion Master Trainer certification to teach a minimum of three classes per week, plus one master class per month. I was on a mission to bring JNL Fusion to as many people as possible so that others could experience the feeling of strength. As I taught class, my clients commented on my changing body. Before I decided to become serious about my body as my billboard, I never thought I'd be able to teach more than one class a day, for fear of not doing better than my clients. Yet after teaching for only a month, I realized I could easily teach a few classes per day. I started seeing my waistline return, I saw shape in my hamstrings, and for the first time I was told I had a body part that others envied. Whoa! What a new feeling!

I continue to work on my body every day with proper nutrition and hydration. I proudly wear my JNL Fusion tanks for every class. I have recruited others to join me in this JNL movement, as well as to attend the next JNL World Conference in 2015. I am a firm believer that if we can share positive experiences with one another, we can tilt the energy of those around us positively, which in turn will spread through the rest of our community.

When I get a text, e-mail, or Facebook message from Jennifer, my heart skips. She has been an amazing mentor who continues to believe in me and the rest of the JNL sisterhood. I am creating my happy ending at the age of forty. I feel more confident, sexy, worthy, positive, and authentically happy, and I can't wipe the silly smile off my face. Jennifer believed in me when it felt as though I was losing myself. Without her guidance and ever-present love, I would not be the woman I am right now. I am eternally grateful for what Jennifer has taught me. My beauty now radiates from within. I believe that we become more beautiful as we find our real selves in life. Beauty is not about the color of your hair, how high your heels are, or even how easily you can get a free drink. I am convinced that true beauty is awarded to mature, caring women in their forties and beyond! Here comes the rest of my life, and I'm thrilled to live it!

CHAPTER TEN

From Bullied to Believing
by Maraya Pearson

Hi, my name is Maraya, and I grew up in a verbally and physically abusive, chaotic, and dysfunctional home because of my mother's volatile and violent behavior disorder. When I left for college at eighteen, I was a ghostly shell of a person with no sense of self-worth due to the toxicity of the environment and the negative beliefs it had instilled in me. Now I'm in my midthirties, and I can say with absolute conviction that my past no longer haunts me. I live in total victory, freedom, and success in every area of my life—and I want to share how I did it. Here's my story.

Way back when, a part of me always knew I was strong, confident, and deserving of love. And I lived that happy, secure truth for a while—until, that is, I reached my elementary-school years and became old enough to become a "threat" to my perpetually troubled mother, who felt it was her job to "bring me down a notch" and make sure I never felt good about myself for any reason at all. Without getting into specifics, let me simply explain that her sadistic nature was nourished by my low opinion of myself. Through tearing me down, she achieved some false sense of power and appeased her intensely insecure nature. Her diseased mind truly believed this was necessary for survival. It was a bullying environment: hostile, aggressive, scary, unloving, unpredictable, and entirely and completely subjugating.

Needless to say, I started my adult life buried in feelings of worthlessness and desperately in need of a rebirth! For me, this process happened in three general stages of labor, so to speak. As with most relationship healings, the first crucial step to my rebirth was achieving physical distance from my abuser through basic financial independence. (Can you sing "Freedom"?) At twenty-two, I'd accomplished this separation by landing a high-paying job; I had a car in my name and owned my own home, which removed me from the toxic environment. Now, several times after my initial "emancipation," my abuser sought to "enmesh" herself with me again, in typical abuser fashion—trying to meddle in my life, my finances, etc. But this time I took hold of my new power, and instead of being a weakling, I simply refused to allow the abuse to happen. In the same way doctors have to cut out gangrene before it kills us, we must take charge of our relationships and cut out all that's dead!

Now, with the "devil" out of the way, God stepped in in a big way to show me the next step toward reconnecting with the echo of my old (real) self. Through a series of "coincidences" and a profound, miraculous healing I personally experienced, this former staunch agnostic, who admittedly thought Christians were weirdos, began a relationship with Christ. As I immersed myself in God's word, I learned about the healing power of grace, and my opinion about myself slowly changed. God's word reminded me that I wasn't a weakling, and that in fact "I can do all things through Christ who strengthens me" (Philippians 4:13).

Although at first I was still skeptical, I took my tiny, mustard-seed-size faith and began challenging my pervasive belief that I was a weakling and that it was impossible or unacceptable to others for me to have physical strength. I joined a gym and tried fitness programs and classes. Soon I began to notice my real self emerging, the one who'd had a natural athletic ability all along. I couldn't help but notice that when I practiced at something, my body had a way of adapting quickly. Although I kept trying to disbelieve it, I slowly allowed myself to see the real me. Within a year I became conditioned for the first time in my life. I could do three straight hours of fitness classes. I competed in a triathlon, finished an intense ninety-day fitness program, and learned how to do pull-ups—something I never saw myself doing. I finally believed that I was indeed strong.

After achieving distance from my bully and then learning through my fitness experiences that I was indeed physically strong, the next step in my transformation required me to address my fragile emotional strength, especially with regard to my relationships. This time I needed to really learn that I was lovable and deserving of love. One day, feeling dismayed over the failure of another lackluster love relationship, a crystal-clear internal voice said distinctly, *"If you think these guys were so great, just wait until you see who I have for you."* I was instantly filled with a pervasive sense of peace, and I no longer feared anything about my future relationships. (Since I tend to be a worrier, this truly was a minimiracle and a real-life example of the "peace that surpasses understanding.") Sure enough, three weeks later, I met my soon-to-be husband. Not only was it love at first sight, we've continued to have the epitome of a happy, healthy relationship. Sure, we have our ups and downs like any other couple, but we have a rock-solid friendship, a steamy love life, and everything in between. As an added and completely unexpected bonus, it turns out that my mother-in-law is absolutely incredible! Not only do I admire her profoundly—she is *the* gentlest and yet emotionally strongest woman I know—but her love and support have brought about a healing and restoration I never could have imagined possible in the area of my broken relationship with my mother.

While the love of my husband and extended family continues to validate my belief in my lovability and to feed my emotional strength, my main love will always be my God, whom I credit with bringing the perfect family into my life. It is his love that is my primary sustainer.

Now that my beliefs about myself, my body, and my relationships have been restored, there is still more victory. As a result of my transformation, I'm now able to give back to others. Since 2008, I've channeled my passion about the influence of the home environment into my website, HealthyHomeCEO.com, which has encouraged thousands of families nationwide and in more than ten countries to achieve a happy, healthy homelife. I authored *The Home CEO's Guide to Life: How to Live in Harmony, Health and Happiness,* which earned a 2012 Living Now Book Awards medal for outstanding nonfiction.

In 2013, my family expanded our impact by adopting an amazing young woman with a troubled past. At one point she didn't think she would graduate from high school, but with the love and support of our balanced family, she has blossomed into an honor-roll, Ivy League-bound student who aspires to become a brain surgeon. She was recently invited to attend an exclusive premed conference in Washington, DC, with Nobel Peace Prize mentors and deans from the world's most prestigious medical schools. We are so proud of her, and the joy we get in witnessing her success is immeasurable.

So for all those out there who have experienced the devastating effects of a bully or an abuser who has tried to rob you of your true self, I simply want to tell you that *they do not get to write the end of the story*! My whole life has been transformed, and yours can be too. Start by getting away. Physical distance is critical. Then, once you are safely away, start to challenge old beliefs until you finally see the truth: that you are strong, lovable, and deserving. As you start to believe the truth, just watch as your story unfolds effortlessly around you. Don't give up! Before you know it, you'll be reborn, and maybe even helping others on their journey, too!

CHAPTER ELEVEN

JNL Gold
by Carol Jean Smit Nowlan

"What the overweight person needs, in order to break out of self-defeat, isn't a new brain, a better metabolic set point, or balanced hormones. The answer doesn't lie in these factors; they are secondary to something else—BALANCE."
—Deepak Chopra and Rudolph Tanzi, Super Brain

If only I had read these words when my world began to spin out of control. But that comes later in my story. I had a childhood to be envied by many, strict but loving parents, a brother sixteen years older than myself, a large loving family, loads of cousins, aunts, and uncles. I was a tomboy, always getting into scrapes, falling out of trees, swinging on ropes. I was a good athlete at school, cross-country being my favourite event. I only became a "lady" in my late teens. I was slim and fit and wore a size 8, and I worked out in the gym twice a week, just to be active. Got married to my childhood sweetheart in 1967, when I was twenty-one. We had known each other from the age of thirteen. You could say these were my "balanced" years.

I fell pregnant immediately. The following year, in March 1968, my son Robi was born. I fell pregnant again soon after. My mother died when Robi was six months old. Her death shook me to the core. I developed asthma. Things had also started going downhill on the marriage front. My husband's behaviour had started changing soon after we married, I was often left alone in the evenings, as there was always some excuse for a boys' night on the town. I later found out this involved other women as well. When my father came to dinner, my husband made sure he left the house on some pretext and only came home in the early hours of the morning. To add fuel to the fire, if I wore something that made me look good, I got slapped and told, "Take it off. I won't have other men looking at you." He would not allow me to go to the gym, as other men trained there. I got verbally abused if I did not have enough cheese on the cauliflower, etc.

The slaps turned into beatings. My second son Dean was born in February 1969, two and a half months premature. As do most women, I was convinced it was something I was doing wrong for my husband to have become the way he was. I exercised at home, as I was determined I would stay in shape. I always made sure I had bathed the children early, done my hair, put on makeup, tried to look like the perfect Stepford wife, to keep him sweet. To no avail. There was no longer any balance.

"Dark times lie ahead of us, and there will be a time when we must choose between what is easy and what is right," says Albus Dumbledore in *Harry Potter*. Living in fear, never knowing when to expect the next bout of abuse—it becomes habit, a way of life. It's easier that way, to stay out of trouble. And so time went by. Four miscarriages and three years later, in April 1973, my daughter Carri-Anne blessed my life. Then fate played a bad card again. My father passed away when she was seven months old. I was devastated. My best friend and confidant was gone. I gained weight, not too much, roughly ten pounds, but enough to be told I was no longer pleasant to look at. I am not going to elaborate, but I will add that after a really horrific abusive incident, I nearly lost my life, and on advice from my doctor, I came to the understanding that I had to "choose between what was easy and what was right." I filed for divorce and ended thirteen years of marriage. My divorce was granted in September 1981.

Most women will think I was out of my mind, but I refused the maintenance the court awarded after six months, because as long as my ex-husband paid maintenance, he felt he had the right to enter our home and abuse us verbally, sometimes lashing out at me with his fists, always asking me or my elder son if I was bringing men home, or if I had a boyfriend. I had to obtain a court order preventing him from doing so. I never stopped my children spending every second weekend with him, or holidaying with him in December. He was their father. I did realise, however, to borrow the words of Eleanor Roosevelt, "No one can make you feel inferior without your permission," which is exactly what I had allowed for thirteen years.

The following six years were indescribably difficult. I worked full time to keep bread on the table, and believe me, we just about kept going. I was not eating properly, I had to ensure my children were getting the nutrition they needed, and yes, I gained more weight. One cannot live on bread alone. My health was none too good either. My asthma was chronic, resulting in many trips to the hospital, to be put on a nebulizer and drip. Result: no exercise…and the rot set in. I guess I may have been a little depressed, but I kept busy with the children's school sports and after-school activities. I did not have time to wallow in self-pity. I neglected my health, and exercise was out of the question. I was far too ill to exercise.

In 1985, Dean had a serious motorcycle accident, almost losing his leg. He spent months in hospital and had six months of intense physiotherapy, creating extra pressure and stress on my already failing body. In September 1986, I was desperately ill. I had no idea I had developed pneumonia. I got home from work in the afternoon and asked Dean to accompany me to the hospital. I was so weak I could hardly walk, and it felt as if I was suffocating. I was admitted to the intensive care unit, where I was put onto a respirator. I spent a total of twenty-one days in intensive care. I was close to death; they did not expect me to survive. I fought every inch of the way. The sight of my anxious children, looking at me through the glass windows of ICU, was enough to encourage me not give up. After leaving ICU, I spent a further two weeks in the general ward. During my recuperation at home, my eldest son was conscripted into the army. South Africa had been engaged in a Bush War for many years, and once young lads had completed school, they were called up for training and sent to protect our borders from terrorists and insurgents.

Another worrying time, as a lot of these young soldiers were being killed.

During these six years I never went out on a date or was interested in meeting men. I was not confident enough, and hated myself for being overweight. I hid my body under caftans and shapeless clothes. I finally realised I had built walls around me, and I disliked the isolation. I decided to pull myself together and join a gym with a friend. Life slowly started looking up. I lost the excess weight, started meditating, and started a new job with a much better salary. Being chronically ill taught me it's not just being overweight that's dangerous. Stress is just as dangerous.

In 1987, I met my soul mate, Alan. We moved in together after a year of dating and married in 1993. We both had good jobs, and life was good. I exercised at home, and we went on regular hikes. The sweat, the time, the devotion, paid off. I was looking good. The Bush War ended. My children were young adults, striking out on their own. Mandela was released from prison and the new South Africa was born. Unfortunately, it became one of the crime capitals of the world. The population retreated behind high razor-wire-topped walls and security doors. Robi met a Canadian girl, got married, had a son and a daughter, and decided he wanted his children to grow up in a country where they did not have to live behind walls and electric fences, and left for Canada with his family. Carri-Anne married shortly after that and within months immigrated to the United Kingdom. Dean followed suit a few months later. He and his wife joined his sister and brother-in-law in London.

Carri-Anne and Dean began nagging us to leave South Africa and join them in the United Kingdom before we too became one of the statistics. Burglaries and murders were escalating in our neighbourhood. Our home was burgled, and we were lucky not to have been killed. That was enough to get us moving. We sold our home and immigrated in 2002, settling in Buckinghamshire. Carri-Anne and Bruce left London and moved to Wales, and a year later my grandson was born. Dean and Vanessa moved to Canada and worked there for two years before returning to the United Kingdom. The recession began, and my husband was one of the unfortunates to become retrenched. Luckily I was not laid off. I had a job with a global finance company and was working in a highly pressurised position.

Needless to say, this lifestyle once again took its toll; over nine years, I piled on the weight again. Alan got meningitis, and we nearly lost him. His recovery was long and difficult. He also developed arthritis, which affected his ability to do certain jobs. He found it very difficult to get work. As a result, when my retirement time arrived at sixty-five, I applied to carry on working and did so until my sixty-seventh birthday. By then, chest pain was a frequent occurrence. In 2013, we moved to Wales to be closer to family. My health and weight once again were a problem, blood pressure was through the roof, and I was finding it was tedious do housework. I weighed in at 231 pounds and had developed angina.

Whilst all the above was going on, Carri-Anne joined a friend at a Zumba class given by Kerry Sanson. Kerry announced she was about to leave for Miami to attend the JNL Fusion World Conference and be certified as a master trainer. When Kerry returned, Carri-Anne was in her element. She loved the JNL Method. All we heard, day after day, was how fantastic the workouts were and how she was enjoying herself.

I watched as she lost weight. Her body started changing in a matter of months. She attended master classes and live online sessions with Jennifer. Soon thereafter, she became an IG media rep and started winning contests. I was becoming interested but was told by my doctors that the fusion exercises were far too strenuous for me. I was gutted. Carri-Anne explained the exercises could be modified to suit my ability, age, and health, and I made up my mind that the pain of being overweight was far worse than the pain of working out. I started exercising. I lost some weight—not much, just enough to whet my appetite for better results.

I heeded my doctors' advice and waited until I had a cardiac angioplasty before starting JNL Fusion, just doing a few of the moves I had watched Carri-Anne do during one of Kerry's master classes. I was hooked. I eased myself into the programme bit by bit, and I have now lost thirty-one pounds! I still have a long way to go, but

I am loving the journey. I have been bitten by the JNL Fusion bug. Jennifer Nicole Lee is an inspiration, a ball of energy, and one of the most positive people I have come across—definitely an inspiration. Her dedication and infectious enthusiasm is second to none, as well as her faith and desire to enable the people around her to become successful too.

Carri-Anne's self-worth has increased a hundredfold. She has blossomed, and in my eyes she is living proof of the self-confidence instilled by Jennifer. She has gone from strength to strength, and the icing on the cake was when she was appointed as Jennifer's executive assistant during the World's 1st Euro Conference in October 2014.

I too have become an IG rep. You will find me at JNLGold, representing the sixty-plus generation. I cannot recommend the JNL Fusion Method enough, and although I am unable, at this stage, to join everybody at the 5th Annual World Conference in Miami in January 2015, the slimmer, trimmer me will certainly be at the 2nd Euro Conference. At almost sixty-nine, I am once again enjoying life to the full. I am most thankful for the opportunity given to me by Jennifer. I am truly blessed. I am the reason why I am overweight. No one made me do it. I did it. I am the reason why I will be slim and fit soon. No one can do it for me. I can do it, and I will do it. Strong is the new skinny. Believe!

I will forever be grateful to my children and husband, who have loved and cherished me through all our trials and tribulations, and have believed in me. How many mothers can say their children (by this I mean forty-something-year-olds), contact them a minimum of once a day and tell her they love her. I can. Take care of your body. It's the only place you have to live in.

CHAPTER TWELVE

Networking: From Trial to Triumph by Aggi Kolodziejczak

My journey started back in 2009, when my fitness studio closed. It was the end of one era but the start of a new one for me. Though I'd invested all my time, money, and energy into keeping my studio open, there were many aspects of my business that I'd neglected, failing to recognize their true importance. I loved seeing my clients progress and helping them reach their fitness goals, but I couldn't see them through their journey because my business was falling apart without my even knowing it. I failed to keep my network active and to market myself.

Determined to learn from my mistakes, I picked up my things and decided to make a new start in a new community. I decided to go back into sales, which was my default talent. I was very good at sales, and I learned that if you're great at something, you should stick to it. From sales I ventured into marketing, learning how sales and marketing work with each other to grow a business. From there I stumbled on networking and the power it can give you.

Whether you're a personal trainer or professional marketing director, at some point in your career you will have to network to create new connections that will help grow your reputation as a professional and make a lasting impression in your community. I've summed up these lessons below.

The Trial and Error of Networking: You Have to Start Somewhere

When I moved to Florida and entered the workforce after owning a business, it was almost like the first day of college. I went into sales for a local newspaper, and one of the requirements was to attend local networking events and parties to promote the newspaper and to meet new contacts who could turn into potential sales. One of the first events I attended was for a local chamber of commerce.

When it comes to networking, I learned very quickly that the first hour is the most productive. The guests are anyone from business owners to local residents who are looking to network and meet new contacts. I have found that making connections with a few people is more effective than trying to connect with everyone in the room. By making just a few initial contacts, you are creating an image of yourself in your community. Make that impression a great one by always being positive and upbeat.

That being said, networking is a form of "business mingling," so be sure to introduce yourself as the professional you are, and be open to learning about the person in front of you. The trial and error of networking means you will make some great connections, while others won't really go anywhere. You might make an effort to network with someone, but there isn't a natural "click." If that happens, it's fine to move on and learn from your experiences. You have to learn what works for you, and the only way to do that is through trial and error.

As you develop your networking style, it's also a good idea to learn from the best. Research networking strategies and seek out real professionals by visiting their websites or Facebook pages. You can learn a lot from professionals by listening to their experiences. Whether it's a YouTube video, a *Forbes* article, or Jennifer Nicole Lee, anyone who has personality and knows how to show it is someone worth learning from. Seeing what works for them can help you develop your own style.

Besides networking parties and events, social media has become one of my favorite ways to network. Sites like Facebook, Twitter, and LinkedIn, to name a few, have all provided me ways to maintain current connections and to make new ones. That being said, making a connection in person is different from making one online. Connecting online is about more than just making a friend request. Go the extra step by introducing yourself, and show the person you're trying to connect with that you're genuinely reaching out to make a professional connection. This has allowed me to make numerous connections, even with celebrities like Jennifer Nicole Lee, top executives, and countless other professionals who respect my connection as I respect theirs.

Keep in mind that not all connections are created equal. Don't underestimate anyone you meet. I always sought to go to the best networking parties, believing they would give me the best leads. But no matter whom you meet, whether it's someone who can do business with you or not, the most important thing is to establish a connection. You never know who might turn out to be a potential lead. Maybe the person will refer business to you or will keep you in mind when he or she does need your services. I have met many professionals who I thought would be great leads, but it turned out to be the person's assistant or some other unexpected connection who led me to other great connections. The bonus of connecting naturally has been meeting new friends who are now part of my network.

Keep Your Homelife at Home and Focus on Your Brand

I can't tell you how many times I've gone to a networking event and met a great new connection only to have him or her lose credibility by bringing up personal problems. We are all human, and we all have some common experiences. But if you need to vent about something, you should do that with a counselor or your support system. Conversations with new connections should always be engaging. You want to give some information about who you are and what you do, but make sure to focus on learning about your new connection. It's natural to meet new friends through networking, but don't forget that your new friend is still a professional connection. If you'd like that connection to be a lasting one, maintain a positive image.

Another aspect of networking that should not be overlooked is the power of giving and receiving referrals. Having networked for more than four years now, I have graduated to master connector. My initial connections have led to further professional relationships, thanks to referrals. When receiving a referral, be grateful, and always thank the person referring you. People who appreciate good things being done for them tend to have more good done to them. It's like the law of attraction—the idea that like energy attracts like energy—working for you. I so enjoy referring people to each other. I can't tell you the satisfaction I get from knowing that I've connected people who are now able to work together and do great things.

Through making strong connections, you will naturally make professional friends who will grow into a closer sister/brotherhood. I call this the inner circle, those professional friends you want to see do well as much as they want to see you do well. I belong to a few of these inner circles, but the one that has grown internationally is my JNL Fusion circle, an elite group of professionals I have met in my networking travels. Not only have they helped me grow professionally, I have had the honor to help them grow as well.

Going back to the law of attraction, here is a quote that sums it all up: "Grateful souls focus on the happiness and abundance present in their lives, and this in turn attracts more abundance and joy toward them" (Stephen Richards, *Think Your Way to Success*).

CHAPTER THIRTEEN

From Wheelchair to Fitness Model by Catherine "Dr. D" Divingian, MS, MBA, PhD

"You people are always trying to get special favors!" The uniformed worker at the airport had no sympathy for me as I struggled to maneuver my wheelchair and balance an awkward duffel bag through San Diego International. It was obvious that he was not going to offer any assistance and that he looked down on me. I wheeled away from him as quickly as possible, my face flushed with embarrassment.

It was one of the most humiliating moments of my life, and I wondered how I'd gotten to that point. I had been injured in military training, and my health had grown worse and worse until I had to rely on a wheelchair to get around. For shorter distances I could use a cane, but regardless, I was no longer the young, vital person I had always thought of myself as being. Instead I was broken, deconditioned, bitter, and miserable. I relied on a shoebox full of drugs to make it through the day, to control the pain, and to counteract the side effects of the toxic medicines.

A few weeks after the airport incident, I was back in San Diego. As I hobbled along with my cane on a beautiful Sunday morning, it occurred to me that I could at least try to take a few steps without it. I was sick of being limited, and I wanted to feel a sense of independence. I was tired of being insulted and of watching the world pass me by. I propped the cane against a tree and hesitantly took a step. To my astonishment, another step soon followed. Those first faltering steps represented my initial journey to freedom. I knew that I would—and could—work to overcome my limitations, literally one step at a time.

I started practicing walking unassisted. When I wasn't undergoing physical therapy, I was doing my own "homework." It was tough, painful, and awkward, but I persisted, maintaining my vision of who I knew I was deep within.

It wasn't long before I knew I would have to taper off the medicines. Soon I was able to wean myself from the prescriptions and ambulate significant distances. I got rid of that shoebox and detoxed from the poisons. I cleaned up my diet, embraced fresh, organic foods, and started losing weight. Soon I returned to weight training. I took it slowly at first, working through the stiffness and pain, gradually increasing weights and range of motion. Then the floodgates opened, and I became passionate about health and wellness. It was addicting to become healthy and vibrant, to feel optimistic and energetic.

At the age of forty-two, I entered my first figure competitions. When I stood on stage, it was as a representative of how people can overcome some of the worst conditions, broadcasting the message of hope. I continued the message through fitness modeling, projecting a fun, fresh, healthy image for those over forty.

These experiences compelled me to pursue fitness and nutrition certifications, as well as a doctorate in health psychology. I became intrigued about the health choices people make, and the different perspectives that separate vibrant individuals from those who have an "illness persona." It became my mission in life to help others discover the path to their potential and to value the gift of wellness.

How does this story apply to you? It's important to know who you really are deep inside. You are not the tired, haggard, sick, unhappy person you might have allowed to creep into your life. You have the same spark and passion that lights those of us who have contributed to this book. Your desire to become that person who can give back to the world is simply waiting to be revealed. You have your own important message to share.

Take as much time as you need to get in touch with that beautiful person. Your most important assignment is to determine exactly what you want to do with your newfound (or rediscovered) health. Be very precise in your goals. Do you want to wear a swimsuit or look great for your reunion? Do you want enough energy to pursue your dreams from morning until night? Will you be able to play with your kids and grandkids? Will you take up a sport or activity that you always wanted to do?

Allow your imagination to run unfettered by any judgment or censure. Be a little kid and have fun experiencing your dreams in your mind's eye. Get in touch with that ideal self. That's really you. It's not a hopeless fantasy. It's the person you have the deepest longing to become, and it's within your reach.

Fill your imagination with every aspect of this delightful vision. See yourself in the mirror and admire your radiant complexion. Feel how light your body has become, the boundless energy that bubbles up out of you, and the bounce in your step. Taste and smell the fresh, light, earthy foods that will nourish your body. Hear the admiration in your child's voice as he or she realizes that you are a role model. Make the vision real and compelling. Once you have that crystal-clear image, hold it in front of you at all times. If you can imagine it, it is already on its way to showing up, so get ready!

Every day, decide to make choices that will help you achieve this goal. Take baby steps, and take your time. Learn what you need to do. Test out new practices, and study how you respond. If you "mess up," learn your lesson, pick yourself up, and refocus on your vision. If you keep pressing on, one day you will look up and realize that you have become that beautiful, vibrant person.

Never give up, and stay strong!

CHAPTER FOURTEEN

Don't Just Dream It, Do It—
Words I Now Live By
by Peggy Caruso

I'm fifty-three, and I finally know what I want to be when I grow up. I also know what I *don't* want to be—someone who looks back on her life and says, "I should have/could have/would have..." I went through a lot to get to this point, and I want to help other women (and men, if they'll let me) make their dreams come true. I want to share my experiences in hopes that I can help others realize that they don't have to just dream it, they can do it!

My road to happiness was a long, bumpy one. I took lots of wrong turns, got lost several times, and hit a few dead ends. But I found my way with the help of many people around me, and I am now living a life I would have never thought possible. I truly believe with all my heart and soul that everything happens for a reason. We might not realize it at the time, but when we look back, we realize that everything that happened was indeed for a reason, and whether good or bad, it all finally makes sense. Now, trust me, when the bad happens, I don't sit back and say to myself, "I am sure this is happening for a reason, and in three years this will all make sense." I'm like most people: during not-so-good times, I might sit on the pity pot and cry the blues. But then someone is put in my path who helps me realize that the not-so-good thing suddenly isn't so bad after all. It is truly amazing.

I have my own business, and I am a divorced mother of two boys—men, as they keep reminding me; Stephen is twenty-three and

Nicholas is twenty-one—as well as one grandson and three dogs, all living together. My main business is selling surveillance video equipment and access control systems to the security industry. While I absolutely love my job, my passion is health and fitness. I got my fitness certifications and now teach a group-fitness class at my local gym. I also compete in fitness competitions, once again proving that no matter what your age, it is never too late to follow your dreams.

Growing up, I was surrounded by loving parents, wonderful grandparents, and my beautiful sister, Christine. I graduated high school in 1979, and because I could not afford college at that time, I started working full time immediately. I started out in a fast-food restaurant, went on to become a bank teller, and then started my career in the audio/video industry. And poof—in what seems like a blink of an eye, here I am, thirty-five years later. Wow! That was fast.

During all those years concentrating on my career, I never lost focus on my health and fitness passion. No matter where I lived, I belonged to the local gym and went there consistently. Until I got pregnant. When I found out I was pregnant with my first son, I was 129 pounds. I stopped going to the gym and found myself eating for four instead of two. My son at birth was ten pounds, two ounces and twenty-one-and-a-half inches long, with a full head of hair. As for me, I was—are you ready?—198 pounds! I was a perfect example of what *not* to do when you are pregnant.

Unfortunately, I didn't learn from my mistake. I lost most of the weight, but not all. When I got pregnant with my second son, I weighed 134. He was born big as well—nine pounds, four ounces, and twenty-two inches long. My weight only shot up to 187. *Hmm, I thought, I'm getting better at this...*even though my weight wasn't much better than the first time around.

OK, so I was done having children, and now it was time to get serious about my weight and health. At that time I was still married. I was an outside sales rep, and I was constantly on the road. It was tough, but I ate as healthfully as possible. I continued to go to the gym, but I was finding it harder and harder.

My husband started to work nights, and I was getting to the gym even less. I also found that my marriage was not what it used to be, and that was harder and harder to deal with. My children's father is one of the hardest-working men I have ever met, and he is a great father. I think that as a couple, we just grew apart, and eventually we found that being apart was better than being together. We got divorced, but we stayed in close proximity to each other for the children's sake.

Although we agreed we couldn't live together anymore, it still was a difficult breakup. It was a very rough time for me and for the children. But we got through it. I started going to the gym more often. My boys were old enough now (eleven and thirteen) so they could come, too. The gym offered a lot of different classes, and one that I can honestly say changed my life was called Dance 'n Funk. It was a cardio class started by a wonderful woman, Syd Berman. She was truly an inspiration to me, and she created a group class experience to which no other can compare. I always loved to dance when I went to clubs and so on, and this class took it to the next level. I arranged my entire schedule around that class, which put me in the gym very often, and that allowed me to try other methods of training. Body Pump, Zumba, kickboxing—you name it, I tried it. I found that I absolutely loved all the classes and the atmosphere of the gym in general. My kids also loved it, because it had a pool and basketball courts. Our lives were great.

During this time, I met a new man at a trade show, and we hit it off. He was from another state, but I wanted to spend time with him, so we started dating long distance. Two years later he moved to New York. In 2009, we married, and he and his son moved into my home. He also started working with me at my company.

The only way I can describe my life with this man is to compare it to movies. *Sleeping with the Enemy* and *The Stepfather* are two that pretty much say it all. If you are familiar with either one, you have a glimpse of what our lives became. If you'd seen me on a movie screen, you would have yelled, "Doesn't she see what's going on?" or "I can't believe she is still with him!" I had blinders on and didn't listen to people around me.

I was told prior to my marriage to him that there might be "issues," but I figured nothing would happen when he was with me.

I was different, wasn't I? I was going to change him. Well…I wasn't, and I didn't. Six years later I found myself in a very emotionally abusive relationship, and when you are in that sort of relationship, you really don't realize what's going on. At least I didn't. The abuser starts out making you feel loved and worshipped, but then little by little, things go wrong, and somehow it's always your fault.

My friends and family know me as an extremely confident, independent, generous, considerate person, one who likes to do things herself and be in control of the situation. I'll admit it, I often don't let others help me, and I tend to do everything myself. So while I was in this relationship, I decided that it was time to let someone else control things for a while. Little did I know what I was getting myself into. Over the next few years, I began to lose myself—my values, my friends, my self-esteem…pretty much everything.

I didn't realize until six years later that every male friend had for one reason or another disappeared from my life, and my time with my girlfriends had become less and less. I was always trying to make my husband happy so he wouldn't be disappointed with me, and I wouldn't "get in trouble" with him. Crazy, right? My self-esteem was down to nothing. I started to separate myself from my friends more and more. Even my business began to suffer. As I grew weaker, he grew stronger. This worked for him in our personal life, but not in the business world and in my company. My business associates began to notice changes in the way things were run, and they weren't happy. They started questioning things. Our sales numbers began to decline, and the worst part was I was letting it happen.

I was a wreck and didn't know what to do. No one knew what was going on. Not my best friends, not my family, not my business associates. I kept everything to myself to protect him, though looking back now, I see it was really to protect me. I felt like a fool. Everyone had been right about him, and I hadn't listened. I was embarrassed and quite frankly didn't want to admit what a big mistake I'd made and that I should have listened to them.

Things continued to get worse. If I didn't let my husband run the business, he would punish me in our personal life. Mind you, he never was physical with me; it was all about verbal abuse. Sometimes

I almost wish it *had* been physical so that people could have seen what was going on and intervened sooner. It sounds crazy, but I felt crazy. When things started to really get out of control, other issues he had came to light. At one point I convinced him to see a therapist with me. I kept telling him our relationship was not right, but if we worked at it and made changes, maybe it would be OK. We saw the same therapist together as well as separately. After only a few sessions, my therapist said to me, "I'm not going to tell you to walk away from this relationship. Put your sneakers on and run."

So I did. I explained what was going on to my family, my friends, and my coworkers—all the people I'd pushed out of my life. All welcomed me back with open arms. They had all known something was going on, but I would not let them in. I didn't want to hear them say I was wrong. Well, you know what? I was wrong. I'd made the biggest mistake of my life. The worst part of it was that my kids were involved and had to live the nightmare with me. There are tears rolling down my face as I am writing this. But these tears are not because I hurt—I've cried those tears many times. These are tears are of joy and gratitude that I was lucky enough to have the support of everyone around me to help me live through this horrible experience and move forward. I picked myself up, and I am stronger and better than before. If there is a woman out there who for one minute feels like she is being mistreated or disrespected, or maybe she isn't sure what she's feeling but knows something in her relationship just doesn't feel right, I urge her to talk to someone about it. Abuse is a serious situation, and I am here to help anyone who needs it.

In 2011, I was free—and I mean *free.* I felt reborn, and I decided never to let anyone or anything keep me from my dreams again. I was getting more and more involved at my gym, and one day I saw a poster in the locker room about a fitness competition. I told no one, but I decided to go check it out as a spectator. I'd always been interested in body building and followed some body builders in magazines and books. I went to the competition and sat in the audience, and I knew immediately I wanted to compete.

So here I was, now fifty years old, thinking about becoming a body builder. Body building doesn't mean you have to get big bulky muscles and look like a man. Body building means building the body you want, and what I wanted was to have well-defined, sculpted muscles. I met with the show's organizers and found that they did one-on-one training at a local training center close to where I lived. I couldn't believe it! I immediately signed on with Mike and Corrie-Beth Lipowski at Pure Physique fitness studio and started to train with Beth Colucci to meet my competition goals. While at Pure Physique, I met a woman who'd started training with a body-building team made up of women just like me. I became a member of Tabitha Sierra's Brick House Bodies, which brought me to yet another level with nutrition and exercise.

Along with the Brick House training, I ventured into different types of group classes as well. In one group Zumba class for cardio, I met Roxanne Thaler, who shared my passion for competing and introduced me to a fitness camp by Monica Brant in Canada. I couldn't believe it—I had been following Monica Brant for many years. So I flew to Canada. While at that camp, I met Jessica Louise Li, who mentioned that she was involved with the most energetic and powerful woman she had ever met, a woman who was running a Fitness Model Factory event in NYC. That woman was Jennifer Nicole Lee. Meeting Jennifer took me to a level I had never thought possible. I went to my first JNL Fitness Factory modeling event, and all I can say is *wow, wow, wow.*

This event changed my life forever. It made me realize that I can go full speed ahead with my passion and that nothing can stop me. The Factory explained how to brand yourself and taught me the ropes of the fitness industry, but more important, it taught me the JNL Fusion method, which got my body to its best shape ever. I loved it so much, I have become a JNL Fusion Master Trainer so that I can share Jennifer's method with anyone who will let me.

I took everything I'd learned and decided it was time to enter fitness/body-building competitions. I am proud to say that at fifty-one years young, I won first place in the Women's Masters Figure category at the 2013 Drug Free Athletes Coalition Pure Physique Natural NY Pro/Am competition. At fifty-two I won first place in the over-fifty category at Laura London's Fit & Fabulous Mom

Contest in Florida, and I took first place in the Classic Figure category at the 2013 International Natural Bodybuilding Federation Northeast Classic in Boston. And I am not done yet! This November, at fifty-three, I will be competing in the 2014 World Beauty Fitness & Fashion Inc. Rhode Island Fitness and Fashion Spectacular.

Three years ago I was thinking I would never be happy again. I had low self-esteem, I was in a rut, and I was headed for disaster. By attending that first dance class and meeting Syd Berman and all the dancers, I kept on going to the gym, which was where I saw that poster advertising body building, which led me to Pure Physique, which led me to Brick House Bodies, which led me to attending a Zumba class and meeting Roxanne, who led me to Monica Brant's event, where I met Jessica, who led me to Jennifer Nicole Lee…and poof! Here I stand, a strong, healthy, confident woman who's ready to take on anything that comes her way…and a woman who knows that every person she meets in her life is there for a reason.

I have been so honored and blessed to have all these wonderful people come into my life. Jennifer has given me opportunities I would have never thought possible: to spread the JNL Method, to attend her Fitness Model Factory events, and to share her passion with every woman of any age, any shape, and any size. It's never too early or too late to start on the road to a healthy lifestyle. I will never forget any of the women I've met along the way. We all have two things in common: a passion for health and fitness, and a passion to share our knowledge.

I truly have never been happier.

Don't just dream it, do it!

CHAPTER FIFTEEN

Got Guts?
by Rae Long

As a freshman in high school, I was young, bubbly, and loving life, but I was unhappy with the body I was living in. My boyfriend and I were at the pool with friends one day, and one of the guys hanging with us made fun of my major jelly belly and noticeable weight gain. I went home that night feeling unsatisfied and shocked at the amount of weight I suddenly realized I'd gained over the past year. I am only five feet tall, and at the time I was forty pounds overweight. That same evening I got online and looked for inspirational photos. That was when I discovered the one and only Jennifer Nicole Lee. Her rock-hard body and defined abs made me eager to change my poor eating habits and begin working out. I even texted all of my friends, telling them I was transforming myself so I could have abs and look fierce. They all laughed, but I was not kidding. I was suddenly passionate about something—fitness. I hung Jennifer's picture on my wall and was determined to create a strong, fit, and defined body.

And that is when it happened.

I was on a roll and toning multiple parts of my body when suddenly, at the beginning of August, I knew something was very wrong. I began to feel sluggish and unable to eat familiar foods without feeling deathly ill. I began to drop pounds without even trying, and my body began to fade as fast as the summer days. As I began my sophomore year of high school, my legs and heart would tire only a few hours into the school day. I was becoming more intolerant of food, and I was petrified. One evening after school, I was lying on the sofa, feeling slow and lifeless. I weighed just eighty-some pounds, with no trace of the muscle I'd built during the summer. My father came over to the sofa to kiss me goodnight, and I told him that I believed my time was coming to an end soon. My body was beginning to shut down.

My parents immediately began researching physicians who could help. They discovered an osteopathic physician in Philadelphia. After one consultation with him, he informed us that I'd tested positive for Lyme disease and needed to undergo two months of intravenous antibiotics. That same evening, on our way home from Philadelphia, my mother woke me up in our family van. The doctor had called to say my heart rate was only thirty-two beats per minute, and they were rushing me to the emergency room.

In the ER, doctors and nurses hovered over me, delicately caressing my frail body. I told them my symptoms: low heart rate, strange sensations inside my stomach, and extreme exhaustion. After blood tests, IV hookups, and an EKG, a nurse entered my room with some paper work, informing my parents that she had good and bad news. Good news: I was not pregnant. Bad news: the doctor strongly recommended I attend a treatment facility for anorexia nervosa. My parents and I looked at each other, utterly confused. Why would the doctors think I was pregnant? And how could they think I was anorexic when normally I ate like a teenage boy going through puberty? My father had even called me his little Shop-Vac! This did not make any sense. My parents decided that I would begin treatments with the physician in Philadelphia for Lyme disease. We ignored the emergency room doctor's recommendations and moved forward. My father pulled me out of school on homebound instruction, and every weekday for the next two months someone drove me to Philadelphia, three hours up and three hours back.

After finally completing two months of antibiotics, I thought I was back on the road to recovery. But this was far from the truth. Before, when I ate, I'd get an upset stomach and could not keep the food down. But after treatment, my allergies heightened to the point where if I even smelled food I was allergic to, I would pass out and turn blue, and my throat would close off completely. I used my EpiPen daily. I went to multiple allergists, all giving unclear answers. One even said that what I had was not real, and if I went home and looked on the Internet for the Food Allergy Network, it would literally change my life. I was disgusted by the lack of respect I was being shown. If physicians did not know what I had, they automatically labeled me as mentally ill because they thought they had to make a diagnosis.

My anaphylactic reactions continued. I was unable to consume milk, corn, nuts, rice, or gluten. (And if you've never noticed, corn is in everything!) I remember going to a movie with my boyfriend and having to leave before we even got into the theater because I had a severe allergic reaction just from smelling the popcorn being popped. Crazy! I was scared, lonely, and tired of all the sickness. I had to live in my own little bubble and was barely able to leave the house. The only thing I had was my schoolwork, an occasional workout if I felt up to it, and a special visit from friends or family.

Months passed, and one day my family and I were gathered in the family room watching *House.* In the episode, a woman was very ill and barely able to function. In the end, Dr. House, being a great genius, saved the woman's life by removing a huge tapeworm from her intestines. I laughed and said, "I bet that is what is wrong with me!" We all laughed together at how absurd that suggestion was.

With my allergies continuing to heighten in sensitivity, and my using over forty EpiPens within two years, my family and I began to search for answers once again. We discovered a doctor near us who treated Lyme patients with severe allergies. I informed the new physician about my current condition and situation. He examined me carefully and took detailed notes. He sat back in his chair and stared at the ceiling. Then suddenly he looked at me and said, "Young lady, I am going on a whim here, but I believe you have a parasite inside you."

The episode of *House* immediately flashed through my mind. I looked over at my father in disgust. The physician said my severe allergies were caused by parasitic damage. I was suffering from leaky gut syndrome, which allows food to pass through small holes in the intestines directly into the bloodstream, causing an allergy to the food molecule being passed through.

To my surprise, a tapeworm was indeed living inside of me, having fed off my food and my body for years. I still wonder how I came into contact with my parasitic creeper. Maybe it met me through my love for sushi, or because I failed to follow my mother's advice years prior about properly washing fruits and vegetables. I'll probably never know.

Healing my body was not an easy process, but two years later, I have finally found the proper natural diet and organic supplementation plan to build a strong body from the inside out. I hope my advice and the supplement line I am creating will assist others who are struggling to get back to a state of good health. I am continuing to strengthen my body with Jennifer Nicole Lee's programs, advice, and inspiration. I feel like a brand-new girl with a new body and a fresh outlook on life.

During my medical journey, I adopted a very negative attitude after being rejected by numerous physicians and isolated from normal activities. I had to learn to believe that the struggle I was enduring was for something great. Understanding now that life does not ask you what you want, but that you can choose how you react to your situation, makes a huge difference. I gained an inner drive that pushes me to remain positive and never give up. I want others to see the light radiating from within me. Life is a gift, and without the help, prayers, and faith of my family, boyfriend, and supporting community, I would not be alive today. I am living proof that you can and will come out of a negative situation stronger than before. What does not kill you makes you stronger, and strong is the new me!

CHAPTER SIXTEEN

You Can! Fight through the Fear to Feel Fantastic by Kerry Sanson

I have been very lucky to have experienced many light-bulb moments in my life. I've been fortunate enough to have traveled, lived abroad, and had two beautiful children. I've made a career as a singer and performer and become a mature student of many subjects, from massage therapy to health psychology.

Despite my changing paths, there have been many consistencies. Health has always been a fundamental drive and passion of mine. I consider myself to be a positive person who is able to adapt to change, something I probably learned from an unsettled childhood.

I can't say I had the easiest time growing up. My parents divorced when I was five, and my father left to start a new family. That may not seem like much nowadays, but back in the 1970s, it wasn't so common. I was different, an anomaly my friends tried to get their heads around. It was tough. My mom worked hard to bring my brother and me up on her own, but for a child, it's impossible to come to terms with why your father is taking care of some other kids and not you. It's a sense of loss that never goes away. I struggled at school, always at the bottom of my grade and always feeling I wasn't good enough.

My mother moved on with her life and met someone else, a man who, although they never married, became like my stepdad. He was a hard man who thought that children should be treated like inferiors and that love was not an emotion children needed to know about. The gap left by my father was filled by someone who could never be a dad.

I've suffered all my life from back pain. At the young age of thirteen, I was diagnosed with rheumatoid arthritis. I was told it was a condition I would just have to live with. No follow-up, no treatment, just get on with it. I didn't believe the diagnosis then, and I know it's not true now.

So what was causing me daily pain? Well, my homelife still wasn't good. My mother was slowly and painfully separating from my step-dad, and I was stressed, insecure, and struggling with studies and my uneasy homelife. This manifested itself physically, and my posture was hunched. Along with all the other growing pains, it wasn't a good time. I remember my PE teacher asking me why I couldn't play netball yet could still take part in dance class. When I think back now, the answer was that you don't feel pain so much when you're engrossed in something you love; self-expression through dance was a passion of mine then and still is. At the time I just knew it felt good to be moving in that way. This was one of my first intuitive insights into how the mind can affect the body and how emotions can manifest in the body.

For the next thirteen years, I tried one therapy after another to help with the back pain—massage therapists, osteopaths, chiropractors. While traveling in San Francisco, I saw a great deal of improvement after a short course of chiropractic treatment, so I signed up for four treatments.

Unlike chiropractors in the United Kingdom, the California chiropractors took a full-length X-ray of my spine and performed a muscle tension analysis. As I sat in the consultation room after my X-ray, my eye was drawn to the two X-rays up on the board, one from the front angle, the other from the side. *Phew*, I thought, *I wouldn't like to be the person with that crooked spine.* Unfortunately, they were my X-rays on the board! Yes, that was my crooked spine, the kind chiropractor informed me as he starting popping my spine back into place. My problem was scoliosis, mild enough to go undetected without X-ray but serious enough to cause muscle imbalance and pain. At least I could see the physical evidence for my years of pain.

However, I was not going to let the problem define me—it wasn't going to be my escape clause. I decided I was going to figure out ways to deal with it and get on with my life. And indeed I did. Within a year I had signed up to study anatomy and physiology and massage therapies.

During 2002, I hit a low point mentally. My job as a singer, performer, and recording artist was tough. The music industry throws a lot of ups and downs at you and challenges your self-worth and belief, and I wasn't dealing with it well. My health took a turn for the worse. I developed an eye infection that was turning into something the doctors could not diagnose. A section of my eye near the tear duct turned red and started to swell, and the inflammation was spreading across my eye. My eyes were constantly bloodshot, inflamed, and angry. It's hard having something wrong with you that is so obvious. Everyone you meet looks you in the eyes, and people couldn't help but comment, "Oh, that looks sore" or, "What's wrong?" Every social interaction drew attention to the problem. I was gripped by unhappiness and fear. I didn't know what was wrong, and no amount of steroid creams helped.

At the same time, I heard about a workshop in the Czech Republic with an incredible gypsy singer I had had the fortune to see perform some years earlier. Her singing had reduced me to tears in one note. The workshop was called Song of My Soul. I decided to take the leap of faith and go, much to the consternation of my mother and the doctors, who were ready to take a biopsy of the swelling and test it for disease. But the only disease I had was with myself and my life.

After an extraordinarily intense ten-day workshop of singing gypsy songs and crying and laughing and crying some more, of exploring darkness and loneliness and wondering if my illness would get worse, I was finally able to let go. I had to trust myself and life that there was strength in me, and to see that it was I who was clinging to the unhappiness and fear. So I let go of the anger, the fear, the fighting with myself. I just let go. I knew then that I would be fine.

Upon my return home, I learned my impending biopsy had been postponed (for which I was more than grateful!) due to other

National Health Service emergencies. The doctors called me in, saying they were worried about me. By now I had been back from the workshop for three weeks. I was feeling so much better about myself, and I had taken to ignoring the eye problem instead of obsessing about it, just cleaning it when necessary and then getting on with life. I wasn't giving it my fear or my anger anymore. I had let go. The eye was responding well and looked and felt much better.

When I went in, the doctor said, "We've been thinking what could be wrong. We're scraping the barrel here, but we're going to test you for leukemia and lymphoma." Great, just two life-threatening diseases, then! I said I was fine now, and it was going away. I briefly mentioned why I thought this was the case, and the doctor's eyes started to roll at my hippie mumbo jumbo. But then he examined me and agreed in a baffled tone that yes, my eye was looking better, and they'd make another appointment in a few weeks. I never went back. The eye problem went away. This epiphany made me think more about how thoughts manifest in the body, and how mental health is as important as physical health. This led to me to undertake a degree and master's in health psychology.

When I first discovered Jennifer and JNL Fusion, I was already searching for something. I knew I had to consolidate all my years of experience as a performer and fitness instructor, my degrees in health psychology, and my certifications in physiology and massage therapies. But I was feeling lost about which direction I should take. I always felt others knew more than I did, so who was I to make a stand? Perhaps those childhood insecurities were still running deep and holding me back. Was I good enough? Did I know enough?

They say that when the student is ready, the teacher will appear—and so she did!

Jennifer's methods checked all the same boxes as mine. Her principles and philosophies were in harmony with the ideology I had developed over the years. The big difference was she was really doing it, living it, and making it happen—making it big, believing, and not holding back! She had belief and faith like I had never seen or heard before. And here she was with open arms, saying, "Come on, learn from me, get experience—come and allow yourself to make your dreams a reality—*I believe in you!*"

This was what I needed. I didn't need any more workshops to take me back to the darkness and analyze why I was the way I was. I had done that, and I will always be eternally grateful for the awakening it gave me. But now I needed someone to help me realize my dreams, to show me how to make it happen. I was ready to climb up!

Michelangelo said, "The greatest danger for most of us is not that our aim is too high and we miss it, but that it is too low and we reach it." It was my time to reach high, set big goals, and go for them instead of playing it safe. I said yes to the conference in Miami, and as soon as I did, the opportunities came flooding in. Jennifer asked me to be a key speaker at the conference. I was overwhelmed. Already I had to face my fears in a very real way. Not just thinking about them, reasoning them out in my mind, but actually overcoming them. Was I good enough? Did I know enough? Surely everyone at the conference would know more than I! What could I have to tell them that they didn't already know? The doubts assailed me, but I couldn't back out. It had happened already—I had taken the first step. I had said yes.

I had to consolidate my training and put my experience to the test. I had to think about what it was that enabled me to speak from a unique and informed perspective. I had to summon the belief in myself that I had something within me that could be important to others. I composed a speech titled "Opportunity." It wasn't easy, but I did it! I took the leap of faith and traveled to Miami, leaving behind my husband, who had been suffering from ill health, and my two young children (hurray for mothers and mothers-in-law for their help!). I went with guilt over leaving my family to follow my dreams. I went there with all my fears and anxieties, with all my memories of childhood rejections—and I did it. I faced my fears. And the conference was fantastic!

I came back with a sense of belief and faith in myself, and I was ready to hit the ground running. I set up my JNL Fusion classes, and my group-fitness ladies loved it—not just the great workout, but all the positive affirmations that come with it: *Believe. Never give up.*

People want this and need this message. What could be better for my students than to come to class after a stressful day's work, to work out and sweat, to hear how great they are and how much I believe in them, and to leave feeling elated and empowered?

One woman from my classes told me she'd been using the JNL Fusion affirmations "Believe you can and you will" and "Never give up" in her job as an elementary school teacher. With these affirmations she was encouraging the children to believe in themselves with their work. Students who had been struggling with math were now showing great improvement, getting better results from these confidence-boosting statements. How amazing to be part of a chain of positive reinforcement, spreading the empowerment to others for them to pass on, too!

Since the conference I have finally set up my business, Sanson Fitness. I'm no longer thinking about it, I'm doing it. I set up a six-week fitness challenge in which I guide people through healthy eating plans, and I use JNL Fusion as the fitness workout for them to follow. I was so nervous setting up the challenge and putting it into practice for the first time, for the same old reasons: Do I know enough? Can I do it? But I did it, I'm still doing it, and I am watching women blossom and become more empowered and confident. It's contagious, and it's a wonderful thing to catch.

I've learned something very special from this experience and from meeting Jennifer. You may never stop doubting whether you can do these things. Doubt is natural, but it doesn't have to disable. It doesn't have to be the strongest force. It doesn't have to stop you from believing. You can choose what defines you. You can start to believe. Once you do, that belief becomes the stronger force. Its power is self-perpetuating. It spreads to others. Believe that you can and that you deserve it, and you will. As Jennifer says, *Believe!*

Thank you, Jennifer. You are a truly inspiring, strong, and beautiful woman.

Be bold, be brave, and reach high. Your dreams might be closer than you think.

CHAPTER SEVENTEEN

Motivation...Hmm...
by Faye Robertson

When Jennifer Nicole Lee asked me to contribute to her book called *When You Are Stuck in a Rut & Need a Motivational Kick in the Butt—READ THIS BOOK!* I was first really honoured but also a little nervous!

Did I have the motivation to do this? Could I push myself to the looming deadline during what was already an extremely busy week for me? Could I get enthusiastic when I was so tired? How would I do this? Why should I even bother? Yep, you can see the irony!

Of course, as a sport and exercise psychology coach as well as a JNL Fusion Master Trainer, I know and understand a little about motivation. However, I have always believed motivation to be a complex and elusive subject. In fact, take a moment to ask yourself these questions:

Do you feel motivated today?
Can you even understand that question?
Can you define motivation?
How does motivation feel?
What can you/do you do to become motivated?
How do you know if you are not motivated?

It's harder than you would imagine to answer these questions, isn't it?

So my chapter may be a little outside the advice you expect. It may be a little unusual or different. But for me, that is what being a JNL Fusion Master Trainer is about. Being different, breaking a few rules, thinking outside the box.

I have written this chapter from the heart. It is not done to show off my knowledge, it is not done to get my name published. It is done because I have been where you are right now, and I know how you feel. I hope it will make a difference, even in a small way, to you. Please take from it whatever you need and whatever suits you.

Here are my three alternative rules to giving yourself a motivational kick in the butt.

1. Don't set goals.
I do not like goal setting. There you go, I have come out and said it.

Contrary to probably every book you will ever read on self-development and life progress, I do not like goal setting! I said it again…

Now I need to justify this statement.

If you are feeling unmotivated, then setting goals is the last thing you want to do. It just makes everything seem harder. Goals require you to take action, to do something, to get up off the sofa, to make decisions. The completion of goals can seem a long way away. Even the best of intentions and the greatest health benefits are often not enough to keep us motivated if they seem far in the future.

So instead, set challenges! And make them in the moment, focus on daily changes, small differences, little improvements. Make sure each day you change one thing, make one thing better than the day before. This may be getting up thirty minutes earlier to have a cleansing hot water and lemon or do your JNL Fusion workout first thing. What a great feeling, boosting your metabolism before your day even starts!

Or read a chapter of your favourite book, have a cup of organic coffee with a friend, prepare a healthful meal, or spend time with your family.

Setting yourself the challenge of making a daily improvement is easily done, and you will find that you feel more motivated to do this each day, because the feeling of achievement will be so fabulous.

Besides, why set yourself goals? You can do anything you want if you (in the words of JNL) BELIEVE! Quite often when we reach our goals we stop, but the aim of this book is for you to keep flying as high as you can, So don't set limiting goals—challenge yourself constantly and see where you end up.

2. Have a bad day.

It is easy to have a bad day. Quite often it is frowned upon. You can't be miserable. You shouldn't feel down or sluggish No, not acceptable. Don't feel like exercising? Fancy a bit of cake? What a crime!

I like bad days. Don't be scared of them. We are human, after all. We are designed to feel a range of emotions, not just the happy ones.

So if you have a bad day, have it. Embrace it, enjoy it. You need it to help you focus and explore problems and issues that are stopping you from feeling motivated.

Comparing our off days to our good days is a great motivator. We naturally want to feel good, so understanding when and why we don't is crucial. Then we can start to deal with and eliminate the things, situations, or people that are making us feel bad and start to move forward.

Just having fewer problems to deal with can be very motivating, as it gives us freedom to do the things that are good for us. There is nothing to hold us back.

And remember, you don't have to be motivated to exercise or eat well. You can still do these things—even on a bad day. A bad day is not an excuse.

3. Inside Out Is Best.

Many of us start a health journey because we are unhappy with what we see on the outside. We are too heavy, our thighs wobble, we don't like our arms or our tummies.

It's really easy to become focused on physical aspects, scrutinizing every inch, every jiggle, and every bit of cellulite. It is very easy to forget that physical changes take time, and progress can be slow. Therefore, start on the inside. Feel the changes happening, don't just watch them.

Health is for the rest of your life, so start enjoying it. Learn to identify feelings of strength, of stamina, of coordination. Relate these things to your life and celebrate when you move that piece of furniture on your own or beat your grandchild in a race or learn to swim or walk to the shops instead of driving. Understand that moving your body feels good, and exercise is a positive addition to your life.

Then health and exercise becomes part of your life. It becomes invaluable, and you won't need to feel motivation. You will just be motivated.

So, these are my rules. I learnt a lot from Jennifer Nicole Lee, lessons that I applied to my own life, and these rules were part of a "code" that turned my health around. Jennifer taught me to believe, to never give up, mainly because she believed in me and refused to let me give up on myself. This seems so simple but was such a vital part of my journey.

I was never alone! And this made me strong.

So, let's chuck another rule in…don't do this alone! You are not alone. Here is my e-mail address: faye@fitgirlfactory.com. Please just drop me a line anytime you want to or need to. I will be there for you, as JNL was there for me. It makes a big difference.

Being a JNL Fusion Master Trainer is important to me. I take it seriously because JNL Fusion turned my health around. As a JNL Fusion Master Trainer, I am here to encourage, to motivate, to support you—my client—in your journey. This journey is not about *me*, it is about *you*. I really hope you take something from my chapter, and I look forward to hearing from you.

Thank you, Jennifer Nicole Lee, for believing in us all. Even those of us whom you don't know yet!

CONCLUSION

First, I would like to thank Jennifer Nicole Lee for asking me to write my story to add to this most inspirational book. I would also like to express how honoured I am to be the one who wrote the conclusion. I cannot express my gratitude enough for this exclusive opportunity. A big thank-you to everyone for their heartfelt inspirational stories; we have all contributed to making this book exactly what it was intended to accomplish. There is no doubt that it is filled with the "world's most inspirational stories."

This book has inspired me even more than I already was, and it has made me realise that everyone has a story that has affected their lives in one way or another. I'm sure it has inspired you, the reader, as much as it has me! Remember that no matter what your life story is, there is a way to overcome it, and the only way is to *believe* and *never give up on YOU*. Thanks to our BOSS LADY who has motivated us to become who we are! I quote from Mr. Matt at the very beginning of this book. He summed up the strength of everyone who contributed a chapter: "Every author, every story could be its own blockbuster movie."

Jennifer Nicole Lee is by far the most inspirational person I know. I have been blessed to connect with Jennifer in ways I never imagined possible. Since JNL Fusion was first introduced to me in March 2014, Jennifer has recognised my work experiences and skills and given me the opportunity of working for and with her, bringing out skills I had given up on, because nobody in my work environment ever took notice of them, and nobody ever *believed* in me. Jennifer is the most generous person I know, and it's absolutely amazing how Jennifer shares her success with all those around her. The JNL Nation is a strong community of like-minded sisters who all want to succeed and become the powerful entrepreneurs they are meant to be, Jennifer being our leading role model empowers us all to our full potential. Jennifer's maxim is "BOSS: Bringing Out Successful Sistas." Believe me Jennifer does not fail at doing this! Those who have already been blessed to join this unique sisterhood know exactly what I am talking about, and those who have yet to join us won't regret it.

I finally had the opportunity to meet our BOSS LADY, in person, in October 2014 at the World's 1st JNL Euro Conference in Canterbury, Kent, United Kingdom. I jumped at the chance to be Jennifer's executive personal assistant throughout her UK tour. This experience in itself was magnificent. Jennifer and I connected in such a way that it opened up many more opportunities for me in the future, where I will continue working with Jennifer and growing with her successfully. So with that said, I would like to elaborate on how powerful this conference was. Not only have I come away with bountiful memories that are absolutely priceless, I have had the pleasure of meeting the one and only creator of the JNL Fusion Method, Jennifer Nicole Lee herself. I've made loads of new friends, opened up many business opportunities, and gained amazing business contacts. If this is something that grabs you, and you are looking to

- meet new priceless contacts,
- gain your JNL Fusion certification,
- work with JNL one on one and with her dream team,
- gain new lifelong fitness friends from around the world,
- finally make your fitness and life's dreams come true,
- have those all-important professional photography shots taken of yourself to build your brand,

then Jennifer's Annual World Conference is a must for you. The World Conference takes place annually in South Beach, Miami, Florida, and you do not have to be a personal trainer, a fitness expert or a fitness model to apply. If you are interested in any of the above, you will need to become JNL Approved, so without delay, apply today at www.jnlworldconference.com.

Jennifer's world conference is not about making money; it's about empowering women. Jennifer wants to awaken the BOSS in *you* so you will be enlightened, encouraged, and educated to be your strongest *you*!

Last, but not least, I would like to reiterate another quote. Marli Resende said, "Jennifer Nicole Lee is known for being a motivational powerhouse." I couldn't have said it better myself, and I am living proof of just how empowering Jennifer is. Jennifer has made me come out of my shell in so many unimaginable ways. I still shake my head in disbelief. But this is a whole other story to tell. Jennifer, I can't thank you enough for just being you! You are an amazing woman who exudes positivity. You are full of life and nothing but fun to be around. Thank you for encouraging all of us to never give up and to never give in, and mostly, to *believe*! Strong really is the new skinny!

Carri-Anne Carmichael,
executive personal assistant
and events co-ordinator
to Jennifer Nicole Lee
aka JNLFusionJunky

ABOUT THE AUTHOR

Jennifer Nicole Lee, the CEO and visionary powerhouse behind JNL Worldwide, Inc., is one of the world's most accomplished super fitness models. An international fitness celebrity, Jennifer is also a best-selling author and highly sought-after spokesmodel, being the name, face, and body of all of her lifestyle brands, wellness products, exercise equipment, DVDs, home products, spa, and digital products. Due to her wildly successful, globally broadcast fitness and wellness programs and key media appearances, she is recognized in over 150 countries. In short, "JNL" is an extremely successful global mega-brand. However, and most important, she is a devoted mother, representing the millions of other moms in the world with a brand they can trust.

"It's my goal and passion to increase the quality of your lifestyle."—JNL

Jennifer's career as a top fitness expert and icon began when she lost over eighty pounds after the births of her children. Her motivational weight-loss success story caught the world's attention after she earned accolades as a professional fitness competitor, holding numerous titles and crowns. She gained international notoriety due to her incredible transformation and was soon a frequent guest on major national programs such as *The Oprah Winfrey Show, Fox and Friends, Extra,* and *The Secret Lives of Women,* and has appeared on E! Entertainment Television. Most recently she was highlighted as the ultimate pitchwoman and presenter on Discovery's *Pitchmen,* showcasing her captivating TV sales power.

Jennifer's energy, creativity, and entrepreneurial spirit, combined with a burning desire to help others, drove her to create the JNL brand. To date, she has appeared on a record-breaking seventy-six magazine covers. In addition, she has authored more than seven books on diet, nutrition, and exercise, some of which have been translated into other languages, including Spanish and German. She is also a frequent contributor to magazines and websites, including *Oxygen, Fitness Rx,* and Bodybuilding.com.

Jennifer is the creator of the accredited and internationally recognized JNL Fusion workout method. Her certified master trainers work in every corner of the globe, providing the most amazing fat-blasting and muscle-toning workouts available.

Some call Jennifer Nicole Lee "the female Donald Trump" due to her uncanny ability to brand, promote, market, and sell with the best. Her passion for business innovation has allowed her to offer lifestyle products and services in the digital realm. Described as "the Steve Jobs of the fitness industry," she has harnessed the unlimited marketing and sales potential of the Internet, creating a plethora of e-commerce sites and dot-coms that rake in a hefty residual income via the web.

Jennifer runs an international consultation firm that has coached thousands of women, and she has hosted weekend fitness retreats that draw women from all over the globe just to meet her and hear her speak. A powerful marketing expert, she has appeared in numerous globally broadcast infomercials for her signature products, including the Ab Circle Pro, Ab Circle Mini, and Chest Magic, as well as on top shopping networks such as QVC and HSN.

Jennifer is the driving force behind the unprecedented success and future potential of JNL Worldwide, which will soon roll out three major lifestyle products, with key television and media spots secured for advertising.

For more information, please visit
www.JNLFitnessStudioOnline.com,
www.JNLMethod.com,
and www.JNLClothing.com.

56054068R00084

Made in the USA
Charleston, SC
10 May 2016